THE YEAR WITHOUT SUMMER

JACK HUNT

DIRECT RESPONSE PUBLISHING

Copyright (c) 2018 by Jack Hunt
Published by Direct Response Publishing

Copyright © 2018 by Jack Hunt

All rights reserved. Direct Response Publishing. No part of this book may be reproduced, scanned, or distributed in any printed or electronic form without permission. Please do not participate in or encourage piracy of copyrighted materials in violation of the author's rights. Purchase only authorized editions.

This eBook is licensed for your personal enjoyment only. This eBook may not be resold. If you would like to share this book with another person, please purchase an additional copy for each person you share it with. If you're reading this book and did not purchase it, or it was not purchased for your use only, then you should return to an online retailer and purchase your own copy. Thank you for respecting the author's work.

The Year Without Summer is a work of fiction. All names, characters, places and incidents either are the product of the author's imagination or used fictitiously. Any resemblance to actual persons, living or dead, events or locales is entirely coincidental.

ISBN: 9781728636009

Also By Jack Hunt

The Renegades
The Renegades 2: Aftermath
The Renegades 3: Fortress
The Renegades 4: Colony
The Renegades 5: United
Mavericks: Hunters Moon
Killing Time
State of Panic
State of Shock
State of Decay
Defiant
Phobia
Anxiety
Strain
Blackout
Darkest Hour
Final Impact
And Many More…

Dedication

For my family.

Prologue

Near Cody, Wyoming

A scream echoed at the mouth of Shoshone Canyon.

Instinctively Logan Miller lifted his head from inside the truck and squinted into the darkness. He smiled as his friend and co-worker Hayden Ryan slung his girlfriend over his shoulder, slapping her ass playfully while threatening to carry her to the water's edge and throw her in.

"Put me down!" Allison yelled repeatedly.

Logan's fiancée Jenna came to Allison's aid.

Hayden glanced back and hollered, "Hey Logan, what do you think?"

He didn't answer.

Logan cranked the volume on the radio before he

hopped out of his black F150 and left the door open so the steady hum of tunes could be heard. They'd been at the quiet spot for the better part of an hour knocking back beers, barbecuing and basking in the warm summer evening. It was a favorite with tourists and locals alike due to its immense beauty. Nearby the sloshing of the Shoshone River beckoned them into its crystal waters while a crescent moon created shadows that danced off the red banks of the 100-mile-long river in Northern Wyoming.

Half an hour later, the aroma of cooked steaks, and pine trees lingered in the air as they sat around the fire pit swapping park ranger stories. And man, did he have a lot to tell. In the eleven years he'd held the position of deputy ranger in Yellowstone National Park, he'd performed all manner of duties from law enforcement, firefighting, and directing traffic around bison jams through to pursuing troublemakers on horseback, pissing on wildfires, saving endangered turtles, and frequently helping lost hikers get home. But by far catching perverts spying on bikini-clad sunbathers was a highlight. It was almost becoming a full-time job. They must have thought that because the park was so vast they could get away with it. Crazy.

"I'm not kidding, it happens all the time. I swear Yellowstone is a magnet for perverts. Isn't that right, Hayden?"

Hayden nodded, taking another swig of his beer and keeping a firm grip on Allison who was draped around him. They were still in the honeymoon phase, unable to keep their hands off each other. Jenna had set them up on a blind date two months ago and for some strange reason Allison took to Hayden's odd sense of humor. For a fellow ranger, Hayden was a wiry man, just shy of thirty years of age, clean shaven, blond, a little over five foot nine and with sharp features. Both of them had always wanted to find a way to be out in the wilderness and get paid for it — being a ranger gave them that experience, and much more.

"I thought you just offered guided tours around the park?" Allison asked.

Hayden chuckled. "No, darling, we are a one-man show covering over 2.2 million acres. Yep, this national park is like a small country. It's a wild ride. Best job in the world though." She leaned in and gave him a kiss. Their slurping noises made Jenna roll her eyes.

"Yeah, if you enjoy being insulted and assaulted," Logan added.

"So it is dangerous?" Allison asked turning to Logan.

Hayden tapped the air with his finger. "Without a doubt. In fact a ranger is twelve times more likely to die on the job than an FBI agent." He said it with a hint of glee, like it was some badge of honor.

Of course he was right but Hayden enjoyed fluffing his feathers and making it seem that it was more glamorous than it really was. The truth was harder to swallow.

"You know what some of the drunk tourists call us?" Logan paused for effect. "The Pine Pigs."

Hayden groaned. "Really, man?" He brought up his index finger and thumb. "I was this close."

By this close, he meant having Allison eating out of his

hand. Her last boyfriend had been with the DEA so Hayden had big boots to fill. Logan laughed and got up to get another beer from the cooler.

"You want another?" he asked Jenna.

She threw up a hand. "Nah, I think I've had enough for one night."

Logan frowned. "It's your vacation. It's okay to have some downtime."

She interlocked her fingers and stretched out her arms. "I'm actually thinking of turning in early."

"Boring. Skinny-dip, anyone?" Hayden bounced Allison off his knee, slapped her butt and she let out a squeal before he began to strip. He tossed his underwear and they landed near Logan's feet.

"Hayden. Seriously?" Logan asked placing his hand playfully over Jenna's eyes.

"She's a big girl. Aren't you, Jenna?"

"Less of the big," she shot back, her lip curling up.

"Besides, it's nothing you haven't seen before, am I right, Jenna?"

"That depends…" Jenna turned to Logan.

Hayden wasn't listening. Neither of them had any modesty. Both Hayden and Allison were already peeling their T-shirts off and stumbling down the steep bank towards the water's edge. Logan remained seated, leaning forward and prodding the fire with a stick. Hot ashes glowed and black smoke spiraled up. The wood popped and crackled. He glanced over to Jenna.

"You never told me what you did was dangerous," she said.

They'd been together for over four years before he'd popped the question. He'd met her while she was camping with a group of friends. One of them had taken a fall in the canyon and the Technical Rescue Team had been called out to get her. Fortunately she only suffered a broken leg and a few minor scratches and bruises.

He shot her a sideways glance. "You've never asked."

There were still so many misconceptions about National Park Rangers and the kind of danger their job placed them in — being assaulted was just one. He just wasn't one to talk about it, unlike Hayden who would exaggerate any chance he got. In the distance they could hear the other two splashing water.

"Come on, guys, the water is warm," Hayden cried out.

Logan jerked his head towards the river. "You want to go?"

"Maybe in a minute." Jenna got up and crouched down beside him placing a hand on top of his back. "You know my father thinks I'm crazy marrying you."

He offered back a confused expression. "Why?"

"Why do you think? You work on top of a ticking time bomb."

He grimaced then laughed. "He's not back to that again, is he? Honestly, you should tell him to treat what he finds online with a healthy dose of skepticism. There is so much misinformation being touted it's unreal. Jenna, the caldera hasn't had a major volcanic eruption in 640,000 years."

"Actually the last was 70,000 years ago," Jenna said.

Logan shook his head. "Okay, my bad. I forgot about the flow that formed the Pitchstone Plateau. But c'mon, it wasn't even close to the one before that."

She opened her mouth as if she was about to say something and Logan beat her to the punch. "And before you say it… yes, the geysers might blow off some water and steam from time to time but that's all it is — water and steam, not magma. In fact if there is going to be an explosion it will be a hydrothermal eruption. Seriously, there's nothing to worry about. The USGS has the place hooked up with all kinds of instruments. And the University of Utah keeps track of all the earthquakes. The first sign of trouble and they'd let us know."

She scoffed. "Like they did the with the last earthquake in 2014. What was that? A 4.8 magnitude."

"Yeah, and nothing happened. Besides it was one out of two thousand that year."

"And what about the 7.2 magnitude in 1959?" Jenna asked.

"Strong, and I admit there were a few casualties with

that one but the caldera didn't erupt."

Jenna stared into the fire. "Still. I can understand why he's worried."

Logan let out a laugh. "We aren't even married yet and he thinks you're going to be widowed. You need to let him know that everything is okay. Yellowstone gets close to 3,000 earthquakes a year and most of them are too small to be felt. It's normal."

"Like Mount St. Helens in the '80s was normal?"

Logan tossed the stick into the fire and turned in his seat.

"Jenna, what's the matter? You having second thoughts about us?"

She was quick to smother that. "No," she said shaking her head and then sighing. "I just worry, that's all. My father wondered if you would consider taking a position on the East Coast on Cape Cod."

He snorted. "Oh, so that's what this is about. He wants you to live near him?"

She stared off into the fire and fine lines formed on her

forehead. "No. Yes. Maybe. I don't know. You know how parents are. They're getting older and want to make sure..." she trailed off. Her parents were good people. Really good. But like anyone worried for their kid, they acted a little paranoid after hearing what he did for a living.

Logan allowed silence to stretch between them.

Jenna stood up and grabbed his hand hoping to lift the mood.

"Come on, let's forget the conversation and go take a swim."

She was quick to change the subject as they made their way down to join the others. By the time they reached the water, Hayden was coming out hobbling and grimacing. He plopped down on a large boulder and began rubbing his ankle.

"You okay, bud?" Logan hollered as they made their way over. He noticed he was bleeding, and had scraped up the bottom of his leg.

Hayden grimaced. "I twisted my ankle and scraped the

damn thing up." He rubbed around the area that was bleeding. "I swear the last time I came here the bottom wasn't this rocky."

Logan looked over to where Allison was serenely floating on her back as Jenna stripped off, flashing her naked butt before running and diving into the water. Both of them looked on, admiring the view.

Hayden puffed out his cheeks and made a sound. "That Jenna of yours. She's a keeper for sure," Hayden said. "Dear me, I swear ten minutes earlier and it might have been me scooping her up."

"Don't get any thoughts," Logan replied with a smile. "Stay here, I'll go grab the med kit."

In his line of work it had become second nature to carry a first-aid kit in his truck. It was nothing special, just the basics like bandages, safety pins, gauze and so on. When he returned he tossed a pair of dark briefs in Hayden's naked lap. "Put these on first before I start treating that leg."

"Cheers, buddy, you're a real Florence Nightingale."

"I've been called many things but that's a first."

They both chuckled as he patched him up. Meanwhile Jenna and Allison were splashing water and having a whale of a time.

"How's it going with Allison?" Logan asked him.

"Ah, it's all right. Not sure she's bring her home to mother material but she's a lot of fun."

Logan was down on one knee finishing up bandaging his ankle. "Be nice to her, Hayden, otherwise you'll bring the wrath of Jenna down on you. And you don't want that."

"Oh no? Do I detect trouble in paradise?"

"No, it's just her old man, you know — fueling her with fear about Yellowstone erupting."

Hayden rolled his eyes. "Again?"

"Yeah but…"

A scream interrupted his train of thought, however this time it didn't sound playful. Logan jerked his head to see Allison screaming and Jenna struggling to remain above the water.

"Jenna!" Logan jumped into action. Without thought to his own safety he hurried down to the water's edge, splashing through the water until he launched himself into the depths. The girls had waded downriver a fair distance. At night it was hard to see as the only light came from the moon and stars. Allison was making her way back to shore, screaming hysterically the closer he got. He hadn't made it within twenty feet from where he'd last seen Jenna go under when he had to stop. The water was heating up, gurgling and burping, roiling up like a Jacuzzi. The smell of sulfurous gas was overwhelming. The river had been referred to as the stinking water or stinking river due to the hydrothermal features that it had at one time. Those had subsided a long time ago, making it rare to see sinkholes or hot springs, or even smell sulfur.

"Jenna!" Logan yelled out her name as he tried to reach her. He couldn't get close because the water was overheating. He could already feel his skin beginning to burn. From the banks of the river Hayden and Allison yelled for him to get out. His eyes scanned the surface of the nearby boiling water one more time before he had no choice but to head back to the safety of the shore. Tears streaked his cheeks as he tried to make sense of what had happened.

But he couldn't.

All he knew was she was gone.

Chapter 1

8 Months Later

Catherine Shaw knew the gravity of danger long before she arrived. Crawling towards the north entrance of Yellowstone National Park, the AWD cherry-red SUV jerked as it came to a grinding stop then started again. There had been bumper-to-bumper tourist traffic for the past forty minutes as campers lined Highway 89 just outside of Gardiner, Montana. It was a quaint little town in the heart of Yellowstone's northern range. She removed her aviator shades to wipe sleep dust out the corner of her eye. Catherine flipped down the sun visor and adjusted her dark, shoulder-length hair. Ahead, she could now see what was causing the jam; a herd of bison had taken up the road. Apparently it was a common sight, that and elk meandering across the rolling landscape. The sky was a deep blue with a few white clouds drifting slowly above the Absaroka, Bridger, Gallatin and Crazy Mountains.

While the vehicle idled, she watched a burly man hop out of his truck and check the connection to his 33-foot Airstream RV. He gave it a kick, and cursed at the thing before getting back inside the cab. She chuckled. She'd considered renting one for the week but opted for a tent as it was cheaper.

She shot a sideways glance to her son Jordan. He had jet-black hair that draped down to his jawline and was sporting a thin long-sleeved shirt, distressed jeans and a pair of white Nikes. His earphones were in and his head rested against the window. She'd told him he would get heatstroke but he refused to listen. Thirteen going on fourteen and he thought he knew everything. It didn't help that his father had filled his head with a bunch of lies about her. They had joint custody but it hadn't come without a battle through the courts. Richard had used his connections as a police officer to try and paint a picture of her being an unfit parent — never around, was the phrase he used. There was a smidgen of truth in it, and of course it had played a role in why they had divorced four years ago but unfit? That was below the belt. She was a damn fine mother, but obviously not up to Richard's standards. Richard's mother had stayed at home while his father worked, so he thought she should do the same. But that wasn't her. Her career as a volcanologist for the U.S. Geological Survey had taken her all over the world. She had worked her ass off to gain the respect of her peers and climb the bureaucratic ladder, and even though she took maternity leave when Jordan was born, she wasn't the type to stay at home fluffing pillows and making sure dinner was on the table at six. But that's not to say she didn't adore her kid.

She gave the truck some more gas and rolled forward a few feet before stopping again. It was Thursday, the middle of July, peak season for Yellowstone National Park and the temperatures were hovering in the high seventies. Catherine reached for the AC and cranked it up as a bead of sweat dripped down her temple.

Finally, in the distance she saw the north entrance ranger booth. It was a log-style cabin with a stone foundation. Snagging up her phone she dialed Richard to let him know they'd arrived safely. He was a stickler for making sure she checked in with him while Jordan was with her. It was one of his many traits that niggled her.

"Oh hey, so we're just approaching the north side. I thought I would call you before we entered as I'm not sure they have much service in the park."

"Already looked into it. There is coverage for fifty percent of the park. So no reason you can't be calling me and keeping me in the loop."

She raised her eyebrows and counted to ten in her head. She hated talking to him as he always made her feel like an idiot.

"How is he?" Richard asked.

Catherine looked at him.

"His usual self."

Jordan began to stir at the sound of her voice.

"Well I told you not to book it. Kids his age have no interest in hiking."

"Yeah, well maybe if you'd taken him camping once in

a while maybe he would."

She heard him scoff on the other end of the line. "Back to that, are we? I think if recall rightly, I was the one that took him to his baseball games, I was the one who showed up at his track meet, and I was the one who actually made it to his middle school graduation."

She narrowed her eyes and felt herself start to overheat. "That's not fair. You know I tried to get back but the flight was cancelled."

"I'm just saying."

"Well don't," Catherine said.

She pulled up to the gate and brought her window down. A park ranger dressed in a dark green jacket asked her what kind of pass she wanted. She told her she'd already booked in advance for Bridge Bay Campground on the southeast side near Yellowstone Lake but had some complications with booking on the north side for a couple of days.

"Not many spots left. It's twenty dollars a night."

While she waited on the ranger for change, Richard

continued.

"Please tell me you didn't wait until the last minute to book?"

"No, I booked in advance, there were just a few complications."

"Which means you winged it."

She sighed. "Anything else you wish to point out?"

He sniffed. "Anyway, make sure he's well fed, and that he stays away from any of the trails with bears."

"Any other marching orders?"

"Yeah, don't go filling his head with horror stories about that supervolcano."

"As if…"

"It's all you ever used to speak about."

"It was my job."

"You didn't have to bring it home."

"Well you don't have to worry about that now, do you?"

"No. No, I don't. Oh, and make sure he doesn't go off the boardwalk. I don't want him falling into any of the hot springs."

"Could you be any more condescending?"

"Sorry?" the ranger replied, thinking she was talking to her.

Catherine motioned to her cell phone and mouthed the words that she was on the phone. The ranger nodded and handed back her change, along with a handful of maps, road construction details and her pass. The truck crawled forward and she heard the sound of a woman's voice in the background. "Who's that, Richard?"

He must have placed his hand over the phone as his voice became muffled. She knew who it was — Victoria. She worked as a police dispatcher. Within a month of her moving out, Vicky, as he liked to call her, moved in, making it pretty obvious that he'd been seeing her prior to their separation.

"Look, I have to go. Phone me tonight," he said.

"Actually it will be a couple of days."

"Tonight," he said in a demanding tone before hanging up.

Such a control freak, she thought. She had a good mind not to bother but that would only lead to another argument and she'd experienced enough of them already. Since leaving a well-paid position with the USGS in California, she'd taken a lower-paid job with the University of Utah, which still allowed her to continue her work monitoring earthquakes and volcanoes, more specifically activity in Yellowstone. Her departure from the USGS was another story entirely, one that Richard would often remind her about.

"Only fifty percent of the park has coverage?" Jordan asked, looking down at his phone as if the world was crumbling in. He'd overheard the conversation.

Catherine smiled. "You won't need it. Look around you, there's so much to see."

"Like bison?" Jordan said before shaking his head. "Next you'll tell me there is no TV."

She glanced at him and pursed her lips.

He cocked his head to one side, loaded with teenage attitude. "Oh you have got to be joking? No TV?"

"Barring two suites in Mammoth Hot Springs Hotel, or using Fishing Bridge RV Park, there are no full hookups and there is no television."

"Then what is there to do?"

"Hike, watch the geysers, see wild animals, go rafting, horseback riding, fishing, heck, you name it, this place offers it."

"Everything?"

She gave a nod. "Yep."

"TV?"

"Okay, smart-ass." She leaned over and nudged him. "Anyway, it will do you some good to put that phone down and take in the sights. Can't be healthy having your face glued to it twenty-four seven."

"When you lived with us you had your face glued to yours."

"That was different. It was part of my job."

"Yeah, I heard that a lot."

"Now you're starting to sound like your father."

She tried to remain upbeat and positive but she

couldn't help get a sinking feeling in her gut that this whole trip was a bad idea. Since divorcing, sharing custody had been tricky. They'd initially been based in Vancouver, Washington so it wasn't a big deal but landing the job with the University of Utah had created some complications and she had to get the court's permission to move. All well and good until it came time to work out the logistics of custody. Realistically, Jordan couldn't spend half of his school year in one state and the rest in another. It would be too difficult, they said. All of which meant a nasty legal battle through the courts before they awarded custody to Richard. Even though she fought them on it, his sway as a police officer and the stability he could offer garnered the favor of the court. She'd considered not taking the job and searching for something in Washington but Jordan had made it pretty clear he wanted to be with his father, and after exiting the USGS, finding something with her specific skill set wasn't easy. Still, their separation hadn't stopped her from seeing Jordan for holidays and vacations. Richard might have been a dick with her but when it came to Jordan, he understood the need for a child to have his mother in his life, and there was no doubt about it, he was a good father. She couldn't fault him on that.

"So we're staying at the hotel?" Jordan asked.

"No, we're camping."

"But you said the hotel has TV."

"Yeah, and it also charges an arm and a leg."

He blew out his cheeks and shook his head. Great, this was shaping up to be the week from hell. The whole reason she was taking him out there was to reconnect, to help him to see that he mattered to her, as the past three years when he visited her he would spend all his time watching movies, texting and pretty much ignoring her. She would have been lying to say that it didn't hurt, and that it hadn't made her question her career decisions. Was it all worth it?

As the truck wound its way south cutting through the mountain range, Catherine glanced at the Gardiner River that ran parallel to the road; it glistened and shimmered.

Now that he was awake, she was hoping to dig into his life and find out what was new, but watching him stick earbuds into his ears made it clear the conversation had ended. If she thought for one second that he was being rude, she would have yanked it out of his ears but she knew he was struggling with the recent arrangements. Not wishing to annoy him, she tapped the media interface console and hit play for a radio interview she'd been meaning to get to.

Robert Preston, a fellow professor at the university, had been interviewed at great length on the recent swarm of quakes and eruptions of Yellowstone's largest active geyser. The quakes had surpassed 1,500 with one of them being a magnitude of 4.4. It was making a lot of people nervous and with the summer season in full swing, tourists traveling to the area were demanding answers.

She tapped the screen a few times to skip through some of the small talk until they got down to discussing the recent activity in the park.

"A new warning has been released in an extensive report

about the dangers of a massive supervolcano like the kind found in Yellowstone National Park, Wyoming. And with the recent activity in the park we've invited Professor Robert Preston from the University of Utah to discuss the threat. But before we get into the nitty-gritty of the questions, we need to put a few things in perspective for our listeners. Now if you've never visited the park, let me give you a clearer idea of what we are talking about. First, you have to understand that Rhode Island and Delaware could fit inside Yellowstone National Park. This is a park that covers over 2,000,000 acres, roughly 3,472 square miles. While it's predominantly in Wyoming, a small area of it stretches into Montana and Idaho. And of course, due to its immense beauty, it attracts over three million tourists a year. That's a lot of people, folks. But as you know, there can't be beauty without a beast. So what about the volcano? Well, what you might not know is that Yellowstone isn't your typical cone-shaped volcano that soars into the clouds. It's actually referred to as a caldera, meaning it's all on ground level and the magma reservoir below the earth's surface is much larger than what was previously thought. In fact, scientists have stated that there is an ocean of molten magma far below the earth that could fill up the Grand Canyon nearly fourteen times over and while scientists believe there is only a 10 percent chance of it erupting — that's more than enough to have people concerned, especially in light of the recent swarm of earthquakes, one of which was a magnitude of 4.4, and another a 2.5."

Jordan popped one earbud out of his ear and frowned. Catherine considered switching it off but she thought it would be good for him to understand what kind of work she did, besides, she'd been meaning to catch up with the interview and it was still a ways until they were at Mammoth Campground.

"What?" she asked, throwing him a sideways glance. "A friend of mine is a guest on a show," she muttered. He eyed her but didn't say anything. They continued to listen as the interviewer went on.

"So how does this compare to an ordinary volcano? Well let's take Mount St. Helens for instance. According to

scientists the debris from that eruption was up to 0.7 cubic miles in volume. A supervolcano such as Yellowstone would be capable of ejecting a volume of 240 cubic miles. So essentially two thousand times the size. The eruption could last for days, weeks, and even years. Now before you all get worried, the USGS has stated that even if Yellowstone was to erupt, it could just be a small incident and not something that would send the entire planet into a nuclear winter. So today we're going to dig in and get some answers. Robert Preston joins us now. He's a research professor of geophysics and geology at the University of Utah, a bestselling author, a former geologist with USGS and is the director of the university's seismograph stations, which monitor earthquakes in Utah and Yellowstone. He has written hundreds of scientific papers and given presentations around the world. Okay, Robert, if you would like to jump in and give our listeners some idea of what we are discussing here."

"Thanks, Ted. I appreciate you having me on the show. Okay, so let's make something very clear here, regardless of what our findings tell us right now, we are talking about a

sleeping giant underneath Yellowstone. If it erupts on the scale of a category 8, it could literally tear its way through the United States. So instead of fifty states in existence we could potentially see that number reduced to thirty."

Ted interjected. "Hold on a second, an eruption could wipe out twenty states? You want to clarify?"

Catherine heard Robert stifle a laugh. Twenty-four years older than her, Robert had been around the block enough times to know how to handle media and blow through the smoke coming from doomsday folks who would have people believe the end of the world was around the corner.

"Look, it's happened before. There are twenty supervolcanoes in the world today. One of them, Tambora, caused the famous year without summer in 1816, which was a global climate change otherwise known as a volcanic winter. The last three eruptions of Yellowstone happened 2.1 million, 1.3 million, and 640,000 years ago and we still have the evidence of these giant eruptions with a forty-mile-wide volcanic depression that cradles most of the national

park. Now even though those dates are close together we don't expect it to erupt again in our lifetime," Robert said.

"I understand but they didn't expect Mount St. Helens to erupt, now did they?" Ted asked.

"That was in 1980 when we didn't have the technology that we do today," Robert replied.

"Okay, well allow me to play devil's advocate for a second. There were signs leading up to the eruption of Mount St. Helens several months in advance and yet nothing was done. With this latest series of earthquakes in Yellowstone, what's to say that we are not already beginning to see the precursory signs? And if we are, why hasn't the media been alerted and the park closed?"

"Ted, that was 1980. The cutting-edge technology that we have today didn't exist back then. Geologists didn't have the information to know the range in which Mount St. Helens could react. But it wasn't just that, there were other factors that came into play, like government officials who didn't extend the danger zone far enough and allowed people to return to their homes. Also bear in mind that the series of

quakes we've had in the park over the last ten to twenty years are unlikely to cause an eruption because swarms are common events in Yellowstone. Most aren't even felt. Think of it as nature's way of breathing."

"Right, but it's a known fact that typical signs prior to an eruption are increased seismicity, changes in surface deformation and changes in the hydrothermal system."

Robert was quick to jump in before Ted flew off the handle and continued to fuel people with fear. *"And Yellowstone Volcano Observatory monitors all of those."*

"Then why didn't anyone alert the public to the recent 4.4 magnitude earthquake or at least put the surrounding towns on high alert?"

"Because what occurred was not out of the ordinary, and it would only cause panic. Listen, if we only see one of those things you mentioned — for instance, just seismic activity, or just a change in the formation of the landscape, or only a change in the hydrothermal — we aren't as concerned as we would be to see all three happening at the same time. And, in the event we do, we have alarms within the system that

would alert us. Ted, you've got to remember that Yellowstone has anywhere from 1,000 to 3,000 earthquakes a year and most of those are in a magnitude of zero or lower."

"So there is nothing to worry about?" Ted asked.

"If there was, you can be sure residents and tourists would know about it by now. From what we can see, these swarms appear to be winding down."

As they continued to go back and forth, Jordan turned to her and she noticed he'd taken his second earbud out. "Hold on a minute, is he saying this is below where we're going camping?"

Catherine nodded.

"Huh, great," he said in a sarcastic manner.

She smirked as she tapped the volume a couple of times so she could hear it better.

"Okay, let's talk worst-case scenario."

"Ted," Robert said.

"Hey, you knew I was going to go there, Robert. You might think it's all smooth sailing now but you're not the one that will have to field an inbox full of questions tomorrow."

Both of them laughed.

"Go ahead then," Robert said.

"I guess we can talk facts all day long but I think what is on everyone's mind is this… If these swarms of quakes are a precursor to an eruption, how much time would anyone have to get out?"

"That depends on the type of eruption and what category it is. It's more likely we'll have an earthquake, or a geyser eruption like the recent one at Steamboat, than something that is volcanic. It's also worth mentioning that the ground has risen and fallen for thousands of years without an eruption. Does that mean it's going to erupt? Or is this rising and falling part of the supervolcano's normal process? There isn't enough data to make an educated guess but here's what we do know. I mentioned the big three eruptions but we have had smaller eruptions since then, one of which was 70,000 years ago but that was mostly lava flow. Of course there are hydrothermal explosions, which can affect areas of a few kilometers in diameter. Then of course there was a strong 7.5-magnitude earthquake in 1959 that led to twenty-eight

deaths. What I'm saying is the smaller ones, which affect only a few meters across, happen only every few years. So there are a number of factors. The next eruption may be moderate with minimal effects outside of Yellowstone. It's these smaller ones that we are trying to predict and prepare for because regular eruptions that put out sulfur can affect the earth's climate."

"Okay, but you're still not answering my question. In fact you are skirting around it. I'm talking about the worst-case scenario — a category VEI 8 eruption."

Robert snorted. "Thinking about that is like envisioning a large asteroid hitting the earth. It could happen, but it's not something you can really plan for or worry about, as the probability of it happening is too low."

"So what you're saying is that nothing that can be done? No means of preparing oneself for this kind of disaster?"

"It depends. Are we talking about a category 8 with no precursor eruptions? Remember, magma buildup would be detectable for weeks, maybe years preceding a major event."

Ted scoffed. "That is if your technology doesn't fail."

"I think it's pretty reliable, Ted."

"It communicates via broadband, does it not?"

"The broadband seismometer, yes. It uses cable. The deformation relies on GPS and we have other means for checking on gas emissions."

"But my point is, even if your technology doesn't fail, the cable or broadband might. I mean I can't count the number of times my Internet service has gone down."

Robert chuckled. "You really are considering the worst-case scenario."

"Better to be safe than sorry."

Robert continued. "Okay, let's say we weren't able to detect the magma build-up, maybe the readings were wrong, or something got overlooked and it was a full eruption. The force could shoot up ash eighteen miles high before expanding outwards for up to 500 miles. A full eruption would cover most of the West and Midwest. However, that's not to say that the East would be safe. Ash would rain down on practically everyone in the United States. If you are anywhere within a hundred miles of the caldera, no, you wouldn't have much time. The eruption itself makes its own wind, which can overcome the prevailing westerly wind. The suddenness and speed of the eruption, and the amount of lava, pumice, gas and ash that would spew, would be fifty times the size of the Krakatoa eruption which killed more than 36,000 people, and 2,500 times more than Mount St. Helens. The scorching hot ash alone would block out sunlight, topple trees, kill crops and wildlife, burn and suffocate humans, collapse roofs, take out the power grid, contaminate water, close airports and continue on through the easterly slipstream for up to 1,000 miles or more very fast. I'm talking about covering six miles in less than three minutes. So if the giant boulders don't kill you, the scorching hot ash will. Now bear in mind that typically a single massive eruption is not likely to happen, more often than not it's comprised of a series of smaller eruptions that would essentially unzip the magma chamber. Basically it wouldn't be pretty. But again as I said, there is always a precursor to these events. We would need to see some impressive earthquakes and swarms."

"You hope," Ted said. "One last thing. Can you provide

any insights on rumors about NASA looking to drill down to release heat from the magma chamber?"

Robert laughed. "You listen to one too many rumors. NASA is not involved in Yellowstone Volcano Observatory and the monitoring at the park. Sure, I work with some NASA scientists but that's related to other volcanoes in the USA."

"Then my sources must be wrong, including National Geographic *as several callers reported talking to NASA employees about it. They said it was all being kept on the down low."*

"You might not want to buy into everything your sources tell you."

Ted grumbled as if he didn't believe him. "Look, thanks for coming on the show. I appreciate it. Let's just hope it never happens."

He continued to rattle on for a few more minutes about basic survival tips, like evacuating if asked and not returning home if your property was in the danger zone; stocking water, food, and medicine; staying inside;

covering your nose and mouth; and avoiding geothermal areas and places with ash. Yeah, it wasn't exactly rocket science but it was something. Catherine switched it off, noticing that Jordan had gone back to listening to his music. As the SUV continued along its path she considered Robert's words and thought about the conversation she'd had with him prior to planning her trip. It wasn't that she disagreed with him. For the most part he was right about people being too paranoid, but like many government agencies, there was the information shared with the public, then there was what was discussed behind closed doors, and that was what bothered her. She had seen the expressions on the faces of colleagues as the swarm of earthquakes increased, she'd heard snippets of conversations with those in the field, and she'd done her own research, wading through historical data and looking over video submitted by amateur geyser watchers who tracked the behavior of Yellowstone's geothermal features.

She looked over to Jordan.

While the trip was about him, she'd be lying to say she wasn't curious to see for herself what was going on. Logging on to a computer website, pouring over website data and sitting in on long teleconference calls could only tell a person so much. If she was honest she missed her job working for the USGS; it had allowed her to get out there, in the field, close up and personal with active locations. It gave her a way to make observations, collect specialized data and save lives.

She gave Jordan a nudge as they veered into Mammoth Campground. Located in high sagebrush above the Gardiner River, tents and RVs were surrounded by junipers and Douglas fir trees. There was a picnic table, a fire pit with a grate, and a large food storage box, which was for sharing. There were five park entrances in two states, and twelve campgrounds with over 2,000 sites. Due to the sheer size of the park, most people would stay in one area then go north or south and stay in another so they could take in the sights. And going from the north to the south of the park wasn't an easy journey. It took anywhere from four to seven hours. Jordan gazed out the window and got a sour expression on his face. "This is it? Where are the bathrooms?"

"They have flush and vault toilets nearby."

"Vault?"

"Yeah, it's one step up from pit toilets."

He snorted. "This place is the pits. And what about showers?"

She thumbed over her shoulder. "Five miles back in Gardiner, or we…"

He threw up a hand. "Bathe in the river?"

She laughed again. "I was about to say we can pay to use the showers in the hotel."

"Tell me again, why we aren't staying there?"

She chuckled and ran a hand over his head. "You will love it. Give it a chance," she said pulling into their spot. Although she had her reservations about the week ahead she was glad to finally spend some time with him, even if it would coincide with other plans.

Chapter 2

Billy Brennan had never been one for rules. He wasn't paying to camp in a designated area, neither was he going to ask permission to wingsuit off Mount Washburn, at an elevation of 10,243 feet. This would be the third year in a row he'd given those chumps in brown uniforms a way to earn their paycheck. In his mind he was doing his civic duty, spicing things up and this year wouldn't be any less than epic.

Many years ago he'd spent the better part of a week being chased all over the national park because they believed he was responsible for the historic Alum Fire that spread across 7,000 acres. He might have enjoyed winding people up but he wasn't a pyromaniac. Anyway, being chased was a blast, a real thrill that only made coming here that much sweeter. Forget joining the sheep lining the highways like good Americans, paying in advance and thanking them for their service. The way he saw it, this was God's country, and no corporate asshole was going to charge him twenty bucks a night for entry. Nope, freedom didn't ask for permission or rely on how much he had in his pocket. He went where he wanted, when he wanted, and how he wanted, and quite frankly, who the hell was going to stop him?

Oh yep, this year he had a few tricks up his sleeve to liven things up.

Fireworks.

Wingsuit flying.

Motocross.

A little bit of wildlife hunting.

And of course sleeping under the stars without a care in the world.

Billy and his pal Wyatt Lehane were standing at the foot of the fire lookout tower on the summit just waiting for the other eight tourists to take a hike down the hill. The staff inside the building, which was manned from mid-June through to the end of fire season, was up in the tower. It had taken them the better part of an hour and a half to trek up a long, winding eight-foot-wide path to reach the top so they were just taking a moment to catch their breath before moving into action.

They had their suits in their backpacks and were waiting for the best moment to whip them out and gear up. They had to plan it just right otherwise they'd find themselves hauled away by the powers that be and probably slapped with a hefty fine.

That was the only challenge with Yellowstone National Park. If it wasn't the park's regular rangers they had to contend with, it was the gunslinging ones. Yellowstone had its own law enforcement, a team of rangers often seen patrolling the park. They dealt with everything: crimes, motor vehicle accidents, complaints of misbehavior and damage. Yep, Billy and Wyatt were all too familiar with them. Fortunately they'd managed to stay one step ahead of them each year. This year would be no different.

"You think he's going to be a problem?" Wyatt asked wiping sweat from his brow and gazing up nonchalantly at the firefighting staff. They weren't liable to catch them as it didn't take long to get ready but they could screw this day up and after that long ass hike, that wasn't happening.

Billy surveyed the area and in particular an over-enthusiastic tourist. "Soon as buddy over there shifts his fat ass, and stops snapping shots of every goddamn thing, we'll head up. Remember, toss the smoke grenade on the far side, it will buy us some time to get our gear on."

Wyatt gave a nod.

They waited for what seemed liked half an hour before the tourist turned and headed back down the path. In the distance they could see more coming up.

"Right, let's do this and fast," Billy said turning towards the entrance of the lookout.

The fire lookout was a rusted shit tin on top of concrete that had been built back in the 1900s to help protect the surrounding forest from wildfires. The lookouts were each manned by a couple of airheads who spent the better part of their day probably smoking weed and jerking off rather than staring out of binoculars. On the bottom floor was a small visitor center and restroom, on the second was an observation deck and the ranger's residence was on the top floor.

Billy squeezed the rusted railing on the observation deck. The warm wind whipped at his shorts and T-shirt. Of course he didn't plan on jumping from there, they were going to climb up to the roof, but first they needed to get the ranger out. He drew in a long breath and relished the moment. It was as much about the lead-up to the jump as it was gliding through the air high above the hilly terrain. They'd jumped from Observation Peak last year and soared over the dying whitebark pines and burned forests, but today's plan was to sweep down over the tops of tourists and scare the shit out of them.

"Breathtaking, isn't it?" Billy said, taking another toke on the joint before crushing it below his boot. "How's it looking, Wyatt?"

"If we're gonna do this, we should do it now. More tourists are coming up the path."

"Go on then," Billy said.

Wyatt pulled out an EG18 high output smoke grenade, popped off the top, gave the wire a pull and tossed it several feet away from the tower. It hit the ground and rolled going over the edge. Within seconds a massive plume of black smoke began to fill the air. They didn't have to alert the ranger inside, he was out of his cubbyhole in no time and hurrying down with a fire extinguisher in hand. Calmly but quickly they yanked their wingsuits out and slipped into them. Billy adjusted the video camera on top of his helmet, making sure it was facing straight. Getting tons of online video views was all part of it. He'd already racked up a nice following with his and Wyatt's antics. People all over the world couldn't wait to tune in to see what crazy stunts they'd perform next.

Billy climbed up the steps, and entered the abandoned post for a quick second to snatch up an uneaten bologna sandwich belonging to the ranger. He took a big chunk out of it and then tossed it before climbing over the metal barrier and vaulting up onto the top of the station. Once both of them were up, they took a quick second to see how buddy was doing down below. They started laughing as they watched him empty an entire extinguisher all over the smoke grenade that was spewing out a large plume.

"Hey fella!" Wyatt yelled. "That's some fine firefighting skills you got there."

The ranger turned, looked up and flashed an expression of surprise before yelling for them to get down.

"What's that? I can't hear you!" Billy said tapping Wyatt on the arm and preparing to launch. They slapped hands, bonked heads and grinned like adolescents even though they were in their late twenties.

"Let's do this." Wyatt tossed back a Red Bull, crushed the can and threw it off the edge almost hitting the ranger who was on his radio, yelling about needing backup and hurrying up to get them. "Let's see if this shit really gives you wings," he said.

Billy replied with a British impersonation of someone from *Downton Abbey*. "Tally-ho, old chap!" he said before taking a few steps back and firing towards the edge. His boots smashed the top of the tower like pistons, before he launched himself off.

Chapter 3

The road was melting. Logan hadn't seen anything like it before. They'd had some pretty hot summers over the years, and he'd witnessed several geysers erupt, causing damage to the landscape and trees, but this was new. He'd got the call late that morning from one of the rangers in the Old Faithful District. There were seven districts in the park and those were divided into thirteen subdistricts, each one had its own ranger station and substation. Not long after losing Jenna eight months ago, he'd taken a position in the law enforcement division of the park. There were several reasons why. It was a step up from his previous position as a general park ranger, it offered greater challenges but more than anything it kept his mind busy, and today was no different.

Leaning back against his white SUV with a green stripe down the side, he jammed a cigarette between his lips, an old habit he'd started again after losing Jenna.

"You think it was caused by the thermal features?" Dave Myers asked.

That was his first hunch, especially in light of recent activity at the park, but they had been told not to jump to conclusions. The last thing they wanted was park rangers acting all paranoid. However, there was a strong possibility that's what had caused it. The park had multiple thermal features: fumaroles that let out steam, hot springs, geysers and mudpots.

Logan didn't reply.

"Well, what do you want us to do?" Myers asked.

He blew smoke out the corner of his mouth surveying the bubbling oil covering a vast area of US-191.

"Didn't they recently lay down new asphalt?" Logan asked.

"Yeah."

"Alright, just give me a minute. I need to speak with the chief."

Logan climbed back into his vehicle and snagged up the radio. It let out a static whine.

"Come in, chief."

As one of two deputy chief rangers operating out of the park's headquarters in Mammoth, Logan handled field operations and reported to the chief ranger who was the head of the Resource and Visitor Protection Branch. Chief Robert McDonald was getting on in years, and those around him could tell. It wasn't just the full head of silver hair, the thick glasses he wore or his terrible taste in music — he'd lost the spark that most rangers had when they started the career. The zeal was gone, and now all that remained was a crusty old man who had lost his sense of humor and would breathe down your neck.

"What is it?" McDonald barked back.

"I'm out on US-191 near Firehole Lake Drive. The road is melting."

He chuckled. "Of course it is. That's what comes from contracting out the work to the lowest bidder. They must have used some substandard asphalt. Damn idiots. I swear this park isn't what it used to be. Do you know, when I came on we ran a tight ship. None of this cutting corners shit."

He rambled on and Logan tuned him out as he looked back at the road.

"Did you hear what I said?" McDonald blurted.

"Yeah, yeah. But it seems a little odd that we haven't had this occur before."

"You mean in all the years you have been working here. We had it before. In fact there was a similar issue with some donated material near Old Faithful that was used to create some of the walkways. It all had to be replaced because it wouldn't hold its shape."

"So you think it's fine?"

He heard McDonald groan in the most condescending way. "Of course, Logan."

"So I'll close off this road until they can get a maintenance crew in here," Logan said.

"Well, that depends. Can vehicles get by?"

"Yeah if they go on the hard shoulder but you can't expect everyone to do that."

"Why not?" McDonald asked.

"Because we're talking about tourists. They're too busy looking at the wilderness."

"Maybe they should be paying attention to where they're driving."

Logan rolled his eyes. It was like talking to a wall. McDonald assumed that if people didn't think like him they were all idiots.

"So?" Logan asked for confirmation.

"Yeah, close it off. I'll get on to maintenance and make sure they don't bring in the same crew again. Geesh! As if I didn't have enough on my plate."

With that he ended the conversation.

Logan slipped out and went around the back of the SUV and began hauling out the signs. Myers gave him a hand.

"This is really going to piss off the public," Myers said.

"Nothing we can do about it."

"Traffic will be a nightmare."

"Myers! Deal with it."

Myers raised his eyes as he plunked down an orange

cone. Logan looked at him and then apologized. "Look, I'm sorry. Just a little on edge today."

"You know, I've been meaning to speak to you. Just… it's never been the right time. I was sorry to hear what happened to Jenna, Logan. She was one of the good ones."

He nodded thinking back to the way she made him feel. The way she could walk into a room and capture the attention of those around her. He couldn't believe she was gone. In the days and weeks after the incident he'd tried to make sense of what had happened. He'd contacted Yellowstone's geologist, Hank Peters, and had him look into the river with the belief that perhaps the caldera beneath the park had moved and increased in size but that idea was dismissed. According to Hank it was nothing more than a transient geologic phenomenon because the water was no longer roiling and the venting had stopped.

Logan didn't believe him.

Although he wasn't one to buy into conspiracy theories, especially about Yellowstone, he couldn't help wonder if the recent multiple earthquakes and the Steamboat Geyser eruption wasn't a sign that the major tectonic plates beneath the earth's surface had shifted. Like many in the park, he was well aware that seismic activity, ground deformation and increased gas outlet at the surface were the three warning signs of an imminent eruption. And despite having disagreed with Jenna's father in the past over the safety and effectiveness of the park's emergency evacuation plan or lack thereof — the truth was the park didn't have one. How could they? The park was too vast. Cell reception was spotty, and besides the twelve campgrounds there were another 300 backcountry campsites scattered throughout the park's 2.2 million acres. It would have been like trying to evacuate a small country. He'd been informed at the beginning of his career that if anyone were to ask about an eruption of the caldera, he was to explain that the YVO (Yellowstone Volcano Observatory) had highly advanced equipment at forty-six stations that would alert them months before it happened. And while he believed the system was effective at monitoring, that didn't mean it was foolproof. Logan thought back to his discussion with Hank.

"Logan, volcanoes are erupting all the time around the USA and most don't cause deaths. We have technology today that gives us warning signs. We've learned from the past and the ones we are watching today are well monitored and our ability to interpret these signals and anticipate future activity is improving. What I'm trying to say is that the chance of the caldera unzipping completely is slim to none. It's more likely to be a small eruption."

"But it's possible."

Hank groaned. "Anything is possible. Look, generally we don't get a warning when it comes to small hydrothermal explosions because water can flash to steam quickly but before a lava flow, there is usually weeks or months of activity. We are talking about lots of earthquakes, tens of thousands, and a considerable amount of ground motion."

Logan replied, "Okay, but that's based on a natural eruption. What if it wasn't natural?"

Hank frowned. "Okay, now you've lost me."

"NASA," Logan interjected.

He chuckled. "What have they got to do with it?"

"C'mon, Hank. I know about the drilling project that the USGS and NASA are working on. It's meant to cool down the magma chamber, right?"

"I don't know where you heard that. NASA has no role in the YVO, or in Yellowstone monitoring."

Logan pursed his lips. "Really? Are you sure about that?"

He paused to give him the opportunity to rethink his answer. Seeing that he wasn't going to expand on it, Logan jumped straight back in. "Then maybe you can explain why NASA's website has an entire section on Yellowstone. It says they are using Landsat satellites to track the caldera's underground heat. The Landsat Program is managed by NASA and the U.S. Geological Survey."

"Well that's news to me."

Logan raised his eyebrows. "Just like the visits we've had over the last year?"

"Those were scientists from the NASA Research Center.

They are doing research into living things."

"Really? And might that also include preparations for drilling?"

He scoffed. "You are reaching. Why don't you leave the study of the caldera to us and you focus on guiding those tourists around the park."

Logan hadn't liked his condescending tone. The information was out there for everyone to see, and there had been enough rumors swirling about scientists from NASA showing up in the park over the past year that it was pretty obvious they weren't there just to study organisms.

"Alright, well at least tell me this. What are the chances of survival if the caldera erupts?"

"Sweet Lord. Drop it. I think you already know. There is no engineering solution to an eruption. Your best bet would be to not be anywhere near here when it does."

"All well and good if you get the heads-up."

"You're overthinking this, Logan. It would take a swarm of thousands, maybe tens of thousands above M5 and those

would have to be concentrated before we start sweating. For example, located in eastern California is the Long Valley Caldera. Back in 1980 there were four M6 events, and three occurred in the same day. Yep, Long Valley has a system just like Yellowstone. But here's the thing... no eruption occurred. Earthquakes, yes, eruption, no. Now back in 2017 there was the Maple Creek swarm here in Yellowstone, which included 2,400 earthquakes between June and September, and one of those was an M4. Lo and behold, we are still here. It's important you understand this, Logan, because otherwise you are going to be like all those gullible people out on the internet writing articles that have no basis in fact. We would need to see thousands upon thousands of earthquakes, many of those would need to be felt, and there would have to be lots of strong ground deformation over a period of days to weeks before we started sweating. Having earthquakes and deformation at a place like Mount St. Helens would be cause for concern but in Yellowstone, it's just par for the course because that's how this system behaves. Every volcano is different and it takes years of studying each of them to understand their patterns of behavior. If we raised an alarm at the first sign of an earthquake it wouldn't just be damaging to the park system, but it would raise trust issues with the public and you know what that can lead to?"

"*Crying wolf?" Logan said.*

"*Ignoring future warnings. You got it. That's why the YVO is monitoring around the clock. You have nothing to worry about, and as for the river boiling, it has nothing to do with the caldera."*

With that said he turned and walked away.

Logan's attention returned to the present.

As Logan finished erecting the remaining sign, he heard a voice come over the radio. "Here, take this, Myers, I'll be right back." He handed off two more cones and strolled over to the truck. He leaned in through the window and scooped up the microphone.

"Go ahead."

"Logan, what's your location?" Hayden asked.

"Near Firehole Falls. Why?"

"I'm on my way to Grand Canyon. We've got a guy

who went over. I've been in contact with Grand Teton for the use of the helicopter but I'll be there before they manage to get the bird in the air."

Yellowstone had its own Grand Canyon, it was located around forty minutes east of him and thirty minutes north of the lake. If a hiker went missing or if someone needed rescuing, the park maintained a dedicated SAR rescue vehicle and had an agreement with Grand Teton National Park for the use of their helicopter and rescue team if need be. The SAR team was mostly made up of park rangers and they had all been trained in wilderness rescue techniques, water rescue and specialized high-angle rescue.

"You got the SAR vehicle?" Logan asked.

"Yep."

He heard Hayden honk his horn. He was doing it either at tourists or bison.

"Anyone else with you?" Logan asked.

"Unfortunately no. It seems those two assholes are back at it again this year. So our guys are trying to track them down. They were last seen wingsuit diving off Mount Washburn. I tell you, man, if get my hands on them, they are toast."

Logan ran a hand over his face and stared out at the vast expanse of Douglas fir trees that lined the road. He already knew whom Hayden was referring to. While the rangers had come close to catching them last year, they always managed to elude them. So when Hayden mentioned Mount Washburn, he knew there were only two guys who had the balls to go wingsuit diving at that location.

Logan grimaced. "Alright, I'm on my way."

He twisted and shouted to Myers. "I've got to go."

"But how do you want me to handle this?"

Myers was still wet behind the ears. He'd only been with the park for a month and so he was still trying to find his feet.

"It's being handled. A maintenance crew will show up soon."

"Soon? Like minutes, hours, days?"

Logan was already in the vehicle and had fired it up. He veered around the melting road and stayed on the hard shoulder gunning the engine. A dry swirling mass of dirt and grit billowed up behind the SUV as he switched on the emergency lights and hit the siren.

Chapter 4

The pale stone of the Grand Canyon cut through Yellowstone's vast greenery. Thousands of tourists flocked to see the spectacular sight that was divided into the Upper, Lower and Crystal Falls. The first large canyon on the Yellowstone River, it was close to twenty-four miles long and three quarters of a mile wide, with depths ranging from 800 to 1,200 feet. Visitors would usually show up at the brink of the lower falls, or head over to Red Rock Point or Artist Point, or position themselves along the South Rim Trail to take photos. When Logan pulled up, Hayden had already brought out ropes and tied them off to a tree and sign. He glanced over the edge and raised his eyebrows. Curious onlookers watched while two more rangers tried to keep them back.

"Is he alive?" Logan asked hurrying over and giving him a hand with the rest of the rope.

"Oh he's alive. Lucky guy dropped twenty-five feet

and landed in a crevice. I expect he's pretty broken up though."

"How did it happen?"

"How do you think?"

Logan shook his head. "Selfie."

"Bingo. Damn guy was trying to take a snapshot of the sign over there when he toppled over the stone barrier. The only reason he didn't die was he managed to brace himself in the crevice down there."

Logan looked over. The sound of water crashing at the bottom of the falls was loud, and a large spray of mist blew up in his face.

"Seems like we were here only last week."

"Seems that way, don't it?" Hayden said. He was all geared up in yellow with a red hard hat on. He had climbing gear over his shoulder and was making sure the ropes were tight. Yellowstone was a notorious place for accidents. Most of them shouldn't have occurred but those that did weren't because of a grizzly or a bison attacking, it was usually people not reading signs, straying from the footpaths or trying to capture a snapshot for their social media accounts.

"You going over?" Logan asked.

"Yeah, I tried dropping the rope down for him to secure it to the pulley system but he's too panicked. I hope that helicopter gets here soon. By the way," he slapped him on the chest, "it's good to see you again, buddy. Haven't heard from you since you took that position."

Logan nodded. "Yeah," he said looking down at the guy below. Their friendship had kind of gone by the wayside since Jenna's death. Hayden blamed himself, saying that he shouldn't have invited them into the water in the first place, but he wasn't to blame, no one was. They'd been there countless times before without issue. It was a freak accident; at least that's what the geologists would say. Still, the strain of losing her made conversation between the two of them tense at times. It might not have been a problem but Hayden kept bringing up the incident and acting all apologetic and Logan just wanted to forget it. It was like reliving a bad nightmare. Even though law enforcement still worked with the general rangers, the move over to that department had made a huge difference. He no longer had to have Hayden ask how he was doing every day, or turn him down when he and Allison invited him for dinner. In truth he felt like a third wheel around them and working with Hayden only served to remind him of that daily.

"So what you been up to?" Hayden asked.

"Let's just get this guy up. Look, stay here, I'll get the rope attached to the pulley and then you can come down and help me get him on the rescue litter. Just make sure you keep a firm hold while I go down."

"You sure?"

Logan nodded.

"You always were better at this."

Logan returned to the rescue truck, slipped into some climbing gear and returned a few minutes later to go over the stone barrier. He began abseiling down the cliff face. Hayden stayed at the top to make sure he was secure until he reached the victim. Down below Logan could hear the man groaning in agony. He looked to be in his early twenties. He had dark hair and was wearing a jean jacket and blue shorts. Logan glanced at his legs that were torn up and bleeding. His girlfriend leaned against the barrier at the top and was sobbing her heart out.

In the distance Logan heard the sound of a chopper.

"Please hurry," the man yelled.

Logan tried to reassure the man while he worked his way down the rocky cliff. "It's okay, sir. We'll have you out of here in no time."

The crash of rushing water far below reminded him that all it took was one slip and Hayden could very well be doing a double rescue. Injuries in the park were on the rise with the introduction of selfie sticks and people trying to capture that unforgettable experience. Sadly twenty-two people had lost their lives and many more had injured themselves, including three employees who jumped into a hot spring at night, thinking it was a small stream. And that was just the ones that were reported. It was common to have people experience thermal burns but not notify anyone. All the incidents he'd been called out to over the years came back to him as a few rocks crumbled away from the rock face and disappeared. Then of course there were the grizzly attacks. Those were nasty. There had been eight since the early 1980s but that didn't dissuade tourists from flocking to the backcountry areas where they were often seen.

The sound of a chopper could be heard closing in on their location.

"How you doing?" Hayden yelled.

Logan gave the thumbs-up. Sweat trickled off his brow as he let more rope out and eased his way down. It didn't take long to reach the guy. He was bracing his body and feet on the opposing sides of the crevice. Below him was a 200-foot drop. A few inches to his right and they would have been bringing him up in a body bag.

"Hey there," Logan said upon reaching him.

"I think I've broken my hip and possibly a rib or two, and…" He motioned with a nod to his left leg where a large chunk of flesh had been torn away

"How do your legs feel?"

"Painful but I don't think they are broken."

"You really are lucky, you know that? What's your name?"

"Jason. Jason White."

"Well Jason, I'll have you out of here in a jiffy but I need to get these ropes and pulleys in place first. You okay there?" Initially Logan kept his distance as he'd seen from past experience how easily people could flip out. Fear had a way of driving people to react in a crazy manner and he couldn't afford any mistakes.

Jason nodded.

Logan inched his way over until he was able to slide a drag and lift harness around him. Because Jason could move his body, it was clear he hadn't injured his spine. Well, that's what Logan was hoping.

"Now I'm going to have to lean you back a bit here."

"Am I going to fall?"

"No. Just take a deep breath."

Logan looked up as he began getting him into the harness. It was tricky because of the crevice. Usually they used these on flat surfaces. Essentially the harness would keep his arms and legs from slipping. His body would press back against the orange stretcher, then Logan would attach a pulley to the top and they'd be able to pull him up without the use of the helicopter.

If Jason had been further down they would have probably brought the helicopter down and hauled him out but they were only twenty-five feet away from the top.

"Alright we got arms in, I just need to secure your legs and…"

Logan felt the cliff face shudder. Small rocks gave away and trickled down like water. He glanced up at Hayden for a second before there was another tremor, this time three times harder than before. An earthquake shook the cliff so violently that Logan lost his footing and both of them slipped down another ten feet. The whine of rope made Logan's heart jump into his throat. Jason let out a loud cry as they dropped and then jolted to a stop. If it hadn't been for Hayden, and another ranger at the top, there was a good chance they would have dropped even further. They slammed against the face of the cliff twice before coming to rest.

"I thought you said I was safe?"

Logan paid no attention to him; instead he placed a hand against the cliff to brace himself, and another around Jason.

"Get us up!" he yelled.

Within minutes they were hauled to the top. The rescue team loaded Jason and his girlfriend into the helicopter and took off for the closest hospital.

"I knew it. Those guys in Grand Teton National Park said this might happen," Hayden said as Logan took a minute or so to catch his breath and slip out of the climbing gear. He didn't immediately respond because his mind was still chewing it over, along with the melted road. Hayden continued. "Logan. Logan! Did you hear me?"

"Yeah." He looked at him and then over to a crowd of tourists who were ushered away by a ranger. "What has Grand Teton got to do with this?"

"I was chatting with a ranger buddy of mine a few days ago. He said that a 100-foot fissure opened up in the rocks over the weekend down there so they've closed off certain areas to the tourists. They think it's related to the caldera."

Grand Teton National Park was a portion of the greater Yellowstone National Park. It was located southwest of Grant Village and it sat on top of a very active magma chamber connected to the supervolcano.

"Why didn't I hear about this?" Logan asked.

Hayden shrugged and looked over the edge. "All I know is we've never felt an earthquake like that before. That bitch was strong." He turned back. "You know, Logan, they say that if this sucker explodes we could be looking at a nuclear winter. It would shower down thousands of miles of volcanic ash and they think it would kill upwards of 87,000 people in the surrounding area and render two-thirds of the United States uninhabitable."

Hayden waited for a response, a reaction, anything.

Logan exhaled hard. "You know cracks in rocks happen all the time with shifts in the tectonic plates."

"Yeah, but when was the last time we felt an earthquake like that?"

It was true. Yellowstone experienced hundreds of earthquakes but most couldn't be felt. On occasion they would feel the earth move but it wasn't as strong as that. Without saying a word, Logan turned and hurried back to his SUV.

"Hey, Logan, where are you going?"

"I need to speak with the park geologist."

"But what about those two airheads?"

Logan jumped into his vehicle and hollered out, "I'll handle it."

Chapter 5

After getting the tent set up, Catherine had been keen to make the most of their time and had arranged to take a self-guided tour on a mile of boardwalk through Mammoth Hot Springs.

"That's right, the hot springs is the only major thermal area outside of the Yellowstone Caldera," the ranger said.

Catherine looked over to find Jordan with his headphones on, and looking down at his phone. She took the phone out of his hands and he pulled off his headphones and frowned. "C'mon, mom, I was this close to breaking my highest score."

"Are you serious?" Catherine asked.

She waved her arms to get him to look at the beauty around them. They were walking along a boardwalk that snaked above the steaming hydrothermal features and provided an incredible view of the travertine terraces. It was a marvel to behold. Water from rain and snow seeped deep into the earth and mixed with carbon dioxide to make a carbonic acid that would rise through the rock and flow down a large terraced hillside leaving calcium carbonate deposited in the form of travertine. The result was a staircase of water rushing down, hissing and steam rising up. All around them the rocks were dry, covered in water, or various shades of white and yellow.

"It's just rocks and water," Jordan said. "I could have brought this up on Google images. Is there anything more interesting to see? And can I get my phone back?"

She laughed and wrapped an arm around his neck as they followed a large crowd of photo-snapping tourists clogging up the wooden boardwalk.

"You know, Jordan, back in my day we didn't have cell phones to entertain us, we actually had to get out and create our own adventure. Seven days. You can live without your phone for seven days."

"Then maybe I should take yours," he replied.

She pulled a face. "Very funny."

He shrugged her arm off his shoulders and moved

ahead, purposefully putting distance between the two of them. *Great.* "C'mon, Jordan." She really thought that once he was away from the noise of California and his phone, he'd embrace the outdoors like she had when she was a kid. Obviously not. His generation had become couch potatoes, choosing games over real life.

"Anyone have any questions?" a female ranger asked.

"Yeah, I do, where is the Internet café?" Jordan asked.

The ranger chuckled. "Kids."

As she turned to answer another question the boardwalk began to shake, and the sound of rumbling could be heard around them. Everyone felt the wood shift beneath their feet. A look of terror spread across the faces of families, and several children began crying. Several people who were unsteady on their feet latched on to the boardwalk for dear life while many screamed thinking it was about to collapse.

The shaking didn't last long but it was powerful enough to trouble the ranger. The moment it stopped, Catherine saw the ranger get on her radio and mutter something. Seconds after, she turned and raised her arms trying to calm everyone.

"It's okay, everyone. Calm down."

"We need to get off here, it's going to explode," a woman cried out, clutching her two young children.

"Ma'am, I can assure you that this is completely normal. In fact you should consider yourselves lucky that you got to witness it. It's very rare that we feel the earth move but it does happen. Remember, everyone, Yellowstone is a living volcano and there are always small earthquakes that cause tremors, and gas to seep from the ground. What you just experienced was the volcano breathing."

"Breathing? Are you kidding me?" a middle-aged man said.

"Sir, the ground surface swells and sinks as gases and fluids move through the volcanic plumbing beneath the park. A few shakes does not mean that it's going to erupt. To date the Yellowstone Volcano Observatory has never seen any warning signs that would lead them to believe an eruption is imminent."

"Not even the fissure down in Grand Teton National Park?" a Chinese man hollered. "My family and I were down there when they closed off areas of the park."

Catherine had heard about that one through the university. Utah was continually monitoring Yellowstone and among the many swarms of earthquakes, the fissure had given them some real cause for concern. In fact it was one of the reasons why she was at the park, in the hopes of speaking with Hank — the park's geologist — that was, if she got a free minute to herself.

Although the ranger tried to keep everyone calm by rehashing historic statistics and facts about how volcanoes react, it did little to alleviate the fears of the crowd. Many people turned and made their way back to the parking lot.

Jordan was one of them. She knew he didn't want to be there and this had given him his ticket out. "I want to leave now," he said in a demanding fashion.

"Okay, we'll head back to camp," she said joining him

and brushing past others, but still keen to capture a few shots before they left. "How about I whip us up some lunch?"

He shook his head.

"Okay, we'll head over to the hotel."

"I mean I want to leave the park today."

She didn't immediately reply to that. The sound of feet kicking up loose rock, and people around them talking about the threat of an eruption dominated. She sighed. "We'll discuss it when we get back."

Jordan whipped around. "I don't want to discuss it. Can't we just leave?"

"Jordan, we just arrived. I've already paid in advance for our campsite. I'm not leaving."

Her cheeks went red as other tourists eavesdropped.

"Then I'll have dad come and pick me up."

"Dad is in California. Don't be unreasonable."

He turned and looked at her. "Unreasonable? Unreasonable is bringing me here without asking me how I felt about it. Unreasonable is spending more time working than being at home."

She stopped walking and looked at him. Behind the teenage angst she could see he was hurting. The divorce hadn't just torn apart her and Richard's relationship, it had formed a wedge in their family, rippled out and affected so much more.

Catherine nodded. "You're right. I should have asked you."

"Yeah, well I just want to go. Can we just go?"

She sighed and put her arm around him and strolled back to the vehicle in silence. Her mind circled around the arguments that had led to her divorce, the nights of tears and trying to come to terms with being single at thirty-six years of age. Although Richard's work in the police and her responsibilities in the USGS had contributed to the divorce, she still had a feeling it would have happened anyway. They had just become two very different people. They no longer laughed at each other's jokes. They rarely sat together when she was at home, and romance, well forget that, that had all but dried up. It was a stark contrast to the way they were when they met in her early twenties. Back then they couldn't keep their hands off each other, or spend more than a few days apart. What had changed? Life. Their careers. Them. It was all kinds of things. They'd tried seeing a counselor and for a while their relationship improved, but it wasn't long before they were back to their old ways. It was just easier to call it a day. Catherine's father had told her that a marriage was never really over until both stopped trying. The problem was, they both had.

On the short journey back to the campground, Catherine contemplated leaving early. The last thing she wanted was to get into an argument with Richard. If it came to light that Jordan wanted to leave and she'd kept him there, he would go ballistic. She was already walking on eggshells. Still, she wasn't going to buckle over one teenage outburst. She wasn't stupid, she knew he would rather be in front of a computer playing games but that wasn't what this was about. It was about them. About bonding. About repairing what the years had torn apart.

She just wasn't sure if this was the best place to do it.

As she chewed over what had happened she noticed a herd of bison moving north at a fast pace away from the park. It wasn't uncommon to see a herd but they were usually grazing at the edge of the road, or slowly crossing and causing traffic jams.

Had it only been that, she might not have given it a second thought except that bison weren't the only ones heading in that direction. Off her to right across the lush green hills, elk were doing the same thing. Had they been spooked by the tremors? Were they just moving to a different location in the park?

* * *

When they made it back, Jordan hopped out and went into the tent. Wanting to keep him occupied, she returned his cell to him. Then Catherine swiped through her contacts until she found the number for Hank Peters, the park's geologist. As the University of Utah was one of the eight agencies that made up the observatory for Yellowstone, and her work involved analyzing seismic data, she was often in contact with Hank. He was an employee of Yellowstone National Park and when he wasn't at home in Bozeman, Montana, he rented a small apartment in the park so he could stay there a few nights a week and not have to drive an hour and a half each way.

The phone rang several times and went straight to voicemail.

"This is Hank Peters. Sorry I missed your call. If you leave your name and number and a brief message I will get back to you as soon as I can."

"Yeah, hey there, Hank. It's Catherine. I'm camping in the park this week and I was hoping to touch base with you to discuss the increase in seismic activity. I'm staying in Mammoth Campground tonight, after that I will be down at Bridge Bay. Give me a call, thanks."

She hung up and stood beside her vehicle clutching her phone as a large flock of birds flew overhead, squawking and heading away from the park. She thought back to the tsunami in 2006 when reports came in of animals escaping and running for high ground just hours before the waves hit. While biologists confirmed that animals had some natural instinct that seemed to tell them when a disaster was about to strike, the officials at the U.S. Geological Survey were skeptical. In attempt to control rumors and avoid panic they had released a statement on their website that made it clear that animal behavior couldn't be used to determine if an earthquake would happen. They wouldn't dismiss cases that had been documented, nor did they address them, instead they opted to sidestep the whole topic and do what any government agency would do to avoid panic — they said their studies had been unable to make a connection. Animal experts disagreed, pointing to a case back in 1989 — the famous San Francisco earthquake — where there had been an increase in missing pets documented.

So was there something to it? Or did it just feed into the public's fears?

As she turned to head over to the tent her phone rang. A quick glance at the caller ID, and she answered. "Hank."

"Catherine. What are you doing in Yellowstone? The university didn't say they were sending anyone."

"A long overdue vacation."

"And yet here you are wanting to discuss seismic activity?"

Jordan stuck his head out of the tent. "Where are the chips?"

"Hold on a second, Hank."

She placed her hand over the phone. "In the trunk." After retrieving them he glanced at her then her phone.

"Just speaking with a friend."

"A work friend?" he asked before disappearing into the tent.

She sighed and got back on the phone. "You sound different."

"Ah, I have a cold."

"Did you feel the quake today?" she asked.

"Yeah. I did."

"And?"

"It's nothing to get worried about. We're on top of it."

"Oh, we're on top of it, alright," she said in jest. "Look, I'd like to stop by and take a look at the data you've collected. Have you taken any samples of acidity in the water?"

"Yes."

"Recently?"

"It's on my to-do list today."

"What about gas emissions?"

He went silent.

"Hank."

Hank sighed. "I'm in the middle of monitoring the gas. Look, if you want to drop by later, by all means, but I don't want you getting all excited. I will admit there have been some changes that are new but nothing right now that would lead us to close the park. I need to do some risk assessment. I don't want to raise the alarm, at least not until I can get a definitive reading from other areas in the park. As you know, it's pretty hard because gases are coming out of everywhere in Yellowstone. It's not like Hawaii where the sources of gas are more focused."

"Alright. Fair enough. When?"

"I have a meeting with the park superintendent tonight at the park headquarters in Mammoth, so if you want to head over there, say around seven. We'll chat then."

"Okay, sounds good."

* * *

After hanging up, Hank wiped sweat from the back of his neck and stepped back from the scene of two dead grizzly bears and their litter. He breathed heavily through a CO_2 gas mask. The animals hadn't been there long as decay hadn't set in, and no other wildlife had feasted upon them, so he was now taking soil samples to check for concentrated levels of carbon dioxide and hydrogen sulfide. CO_2 was odorless but H_2S had a distinctive smell that was like rotten eggs. Most of the gases emitted in the park were harmless, nothing more than vapor, but in light of the recent activity there was a chance that toxic gases were being released. Concentrated enough, those gases were proven to be lethal. Hank stood in Death Gulch, just west of Canyon Village, after being alerted to it by a ranger who'd been out there to find a couple of tourists that had strayed from the designated paths.

After taking samples from the ground, and a few gas readings, he crouched down and ran a hand around the back of his neck. His pulse sped up as he contemplated what it all meant.

"God help us."

Chapter 6

The pristine waters of Yellowstone Lake glistened beneath the afternoon sun as twenty-nine-year-old Darryl Keller stepped into the Bayrunner eighteen-foot rental motorboat. He'd been looking forward to the getaway for close to three years. Since starting his own advertising business he'd put in close to sixty hours a week and the exhaustion had finally caught up with him. It didn't help that his wife, Joyce, was no longer working due to having their first baby, and had made it clear that she didn't want to return to her job as a caregiver but wished to stay home to raise their child. While they weren't hurting for cash, not having that extra income certainly put all the pressure on him to work harder.

Darryl extended a hand to help Joyce into the boat. She was carrying Isabel, their two-year-old daughter. Joyce was in her late twenties, blond with icy blue eyes and petite in size. Although all of them were wearing life jackets, Joyce was nervous about taking Isabel out.

"Are you sure about this?"

"Trust me, it will be fine. Just keep a good hold on her."

The boat bobbed and wobbled beneath their feet as Joyce took a seat at the front of the boat. Isabel jabbed out her stubby little finger and said, "Fish."

"That's right. We're going fishing," Joyce said.

It had taken a lot of pressure from Joyce to get Darryl to take a vacation. But after a number of health issues, and urging by his brother, he caved in. They had brought their Slipstream RV and were staying in the Fishing Bridge campsite just east of Bridge Bay Campground. Joyce had made it clear from the get-go that she didn't like the idea of camping because of the bugs and wildlife. It really wasn't her thing. She wanted to head south, take in the sunshine and beaches, and stroll along the boardwalks of the Florida Keys. Darryl on the other hand had grown up in the woods. From an early age his father had taken him and his brother out camping. It was in his blood and the thought of being cooped up in some fancy resort down in Florida really didn't appeal to him. His idea of relaxing was hanging a fishing line in the water, drinking a couple of beers, smoking a cigar and roasting s'mores over a fire. After a lot of disagreements Joyce finally came around to the idea.

"Just smell that fresh air."

"Okay, don't rub it in," Joyce said as Darryl stepped back onto the dock to grab his fishing tackle. "I still think the Hilton would have been nicer." She swatted away a few mosquitos buzzing around her head.

"Joyce, there is plenty of time to do that. I want to teach Isabel how to fish."

"At age two?"

"The earlier the better. My father took me when I was four years old."

"Bo also put a gun in your hand at eight. And I don't have to remind you how that worked out."

He snorted. "Seriously, do you think I would put a gun in her hand at this age?"

She raised an eyebrow.

"Of course not, I'd at least wait until she was nine." He started laughing and Joyce slapped the back of his legs playfully. "Alright, let's fire up this beauty and get fishing. Hey, did you know that Yellowstone Lake has the largest population of wild cutthroat trout in North America? And the weird part is that scientists didn't know how these fish from the Pacific Ocean got trapped in the lake until recently."

The motor growled to life and churned up the water behind the boat. Joyce was wiping ice cream away from Isabel's mouth and half listening to him.

"Yeah, it seems they now believe that the lake drained into the Pacific Ocean through Outlet Canyon and Snake River and that somehow the fish made it across the divide at Two Ocean Pass."

"Is that so?" She raised an eyebrow.

"Yep," he said steering them out.

"Riveting," Joyce said sarcastically.

Darryl eyed her through slit eyes and his lip curled up.

"You know we could have gone to Florida."

She chuckled. "Please, I would have had to hear you bellyaching about it every hour of the day."

"Hey, c'mon now. I told you that I wasn't set on coming here. I was quite willing to go anywhere you wanted as long as I got a break."

"A break. Will you be taking a break while you're here or logging on to your computer?"

He swallowed hard realizing that she'd found his laptop that he'd stashed beneath their clothes in one of the RV's drawers. He shot her a sideways glance and gritted his teeth, preparing himself for the earful he was about to get.

"Oh yeah, I know you tried to slip that one by me."

"It's just in case clients want to contact me. I can quickly reply to their emails."

"You're on vacation. Couldn't you have set up one of those autoreplies like everyone else does?"

"Joyce, sweetheart, it's too impersonal. The only reason I'm able to land these clients is because I get back to them fast. If I don't stay on top of this they will go elsewhere and then I'll be scrambling for new clients when we get back and I would prefer to at least have some work set up for when I return."

"So you're not really taking a vacation?"

He groaned as the boat slid effortlessly through the calm waters.

"I'm here, aren't I?"

"Are you?"

"Seriously, I'm screwed if I do, and screwed if I don't. Give me a break."

"Darryl. If it wasn't for me we wouldn't even be here. You would still be stuck in that basement working on projects and moaning about how tired and overworked you are. Do you know how that makes me feel?"

He shrugged so she continued, "Like crap. Since I left my job you have made me feel like less of a person."

"Oh really? What, so you're going to spin this back on me? Am I to blame for your decision to stay at home with Isabel?"

"It was that or put her in child care as you are too busy with your work."

"I told you I could look after her."

"Sticking her in front of the TV while you work downstairs is not my idea of taking care of her."

He sighed. He hated arguing. They'd been married for just over eight years but in the past three years their relationship had become rocky. Joyce blamed it on him working all the time but what was he meant to do? He would have loved to sit around doing nothing all day but that didn't pay the bills. She wanted to have her cake and eat it too. Since giving birth her emotions were all out of whack. He suggested that maybe she was suffering from postpartum depression but obviously that was the wrong thing to say. She flew off the handle and spent two days at her mother's house after that argument. Since that day she'd bite his head off anytime he said anything about the house being messy or her not taking care of herself. *"How am I supposed to look after the baby and do all of that?"* she asked.

"The same way that I work ten hours, and do all of that."

The words slipped out and he immediately regretted them. The number of times he'd put his foot in his mouth were countless. It wasn't like he wanted to start a war but the stress of his job had built up over time and he wasn't the best at communicating — neither of them were. They were both as stubborn as one another.

Water sprayed up and a light mist hit his face. "Look, I don't want to argue, Joyce. Can we just have a few hours where we don't talk about what is going wrong in our relationship?"

"Fine," she said, turning away.

He rolled his eyes. It seemed that even trying to prevent an argument was the wrong thing to do. He tried to push negative thoughts to one side, if only for his own sake. Darryl guided the boat out into the middle of the lake and then killed the motor. Joyce sat at the front of the boat with a permanent scowl on her face. It only changed when Isabel kissed her on the cheek. Isabel was good for them. That little girl kept them from letting the small things of life take control. Over the course of the next twenty minutes he cast out a line, and settled back to take in the sights. The lake itself was above sea level, it was 20 miles long and 14 miles wide, with over 140 miles of shoreline, some of which was made up of beaches. They could see other fishing boats on the water, and families playing by the shore. He squinted into the bright sky as a flock of birds wheeled overhead. Even though it was the middle of summer, there wasn't any swimming in the lake because of its extremely cold temperatures that hovered around 41 degrees Fahrenheit. Darryl had overheard a ranger patrolling nearby advise a family that it was probably best not to swim but if they wanted to wade into the water they could. So of course a few brave souls ventured in up to their knees but soon hurried back to the warmth of the shore.

"Did you pack the sun cream?" Joyce asked, as she looked through her baby bag.

"I thought you told me to put it on the counter."

"No, I said put it in the bag." She groaned. "Well we

can't be out here long then."

"But we just got out here."

"Do you want Isabel to burn?"

"Just cover her up, she'll be fine," he said.

"Just put her in front of the TV, she'll be fine," Joyce replied.

His chin dipped. "Didn't we just agree not to argue?"

Joyce rolled her eyes and fished into the bag for some sandwiches. She tossed a bacon and lettuce wrap on his lap. "Here, eat that and don't choke."

He laughed, and then she looked at him and smiled. It didn't last. "Darryl. Do you think it's safe here?"

"Of course. We've got life jackets and…"

"No, I don't mean that. I mean here, in Yellowstone. Earlier on, that quake—"

"Joyce, relax. Turn on the radio and sit back and read your book. You said you wanted to get through it," he said before peeling off the foil around the wrap. He took a deep bite and looked across the lake. Joyce got comfy on the cushions in the boat. She leaned back with Isabel in the crook of her arm and a mystery novel in the other hand. Small waves, barely noticeable, lapped against the sides of the boat, lulling them into a peaceful state. A deep blue sky with hardly any clouds stretched out over the dense pine trees. Another fishing boat churned up the water as it passed by. The skipper waved and Darryl gave a nod back. This was what it was all about. Nothing but blue skies, pristine waters and—

He felt a tug on the line. Darryl shot upright. "Hey, hey, I got one." He began tugging on the handle and reeling it in. Within seconds, a trout emerged from the water flapping around. Isabel let out a squeal as Darryl hauled it in and dumped it into a bucket of water. "Oh we are going to eat like kings tonight."

"Fish. Fish," Isabel cried out.

"Yep, daddy just caught a big one," Joyce said.

"Joyce, I'm feeling good about this. Let's see if I can catch a dozen before the afternoon is over."

He cast his line back into the water and pulled down his Nike cap over his thick brown curly hair, and settled back with his wrap. A few crumbs dropped into his lap and he brushed them off. At his age, a dad bod had replaced his athletic college abs as his personal trainer liked to call it. It wasn't something he was proud of so he would usually wear loose-fitting clothing to cover it up. It came from drinking one too many beers on the weekend, and an unhealthy habit of buying a donut with his daily coffee.

As he was cleaning off the crumbs, Isabel started yammering away.

"Fish. Fish."

He didn't look at her; neither did he look out at the water, as he was too busy digging into his tackle box looking for a specific lure. Darryl assumed she was still excited over his last catch as his fish bite alarm system would have alerted him with a sound if he'd caught something.

"Darryl," Joyce said in a low voice.

"Yeah, hold on, I'm just..."

"Darryl."

"What?"

He looked up and his eyes widened. Hundreds, maybe thousands of dead fish were bobbing along the surface of the water. He turned in his seat and his jaw went slack. For as far as the eye could see fish covered the lake. Other people fishing on the lake were standing in their boats and looking out in utter shock and disbelief. "What the…?"

Darryl leaned over the boat to reach down and pick one up. As he slid his hand into the water, he immediately withdrew it. What had been extremely cold only minutes earlier was now warm. It was like placing his hand into a lukewarm bath.

Fish continued to emerge, none were alive.

He'd never seen anything like it in his life.

"Darryl, take us back to shore."

"Okay, okay." He didn't hesitate to fire up the motor and turn the boat around. Dead fish slapped around in the motor's blades as he guided it through the watery graveyard. They were roughly two hundred yards from the shore when a sudden surge of water beneath them caused the boat to rise as if lifted by a giant wave. Joyce let out a scream and Isabel started crying.

Clutching the side of the boat for dear life, Darryl watched in horror as the lake water rose and surged forward, sending their boat heading for the sandy shore. It happened so fast. He felt his stomach catch in his throat as he lost control and the waters carried them. One minute they felt themselves being lifted, and the next the water dropped out and they found themselves beached and the water withdrawing over the banks and back into the lake.

Both of them hopped out of the boat and turned to see several boats capsized, and people splashing around in the fish-infested waters. Rangers frantically jumped into action, some told people to get back from the lake, others got on their radios and a couple hopped into a boat to try and help those washed overboard.

Many tourists stood by aimlessly in utter disbelief as fish washed up on the beach, and areas of the lake began to bubble, letting off steam into the atmosphere.

It was like something out of a biblical plague.

A horror unlike anything he could have imagined.

Darryl rushed to help but rangers were ordering people to head back to their campsites until further instructions.

Chapter 7

"You think they're gone?" Wyatt said from their shrouded position in the forest. The wingsuit jump had been a complete success. It was an adrenaline rush that not even an orgasm could come close to. Nothing was like the thrill of flying through the air and feeling the wind whipping at their suits. Scaring the shit out of tourists and pissing off the rangers was just the icing on the cake. They'd landed just north of Yellowstone Lake in what was known as Elephant Back Mountain. Earlier that day, they'd set up camp near Dryad Lake, a thirty-eight acre oasis that was off the beaten path in an area of Yellowstone that was rarely frequented by hikers. It was like having their very own private getaway. Every year they changed location to keep the rangers on their toes and this year was no different. Billy was well aware of the consequences of getting caught and that's why they'd opted for an isolated area where they weren't far from the convenience of Bridge Bay campground but far enough that they could hop on their dirt bikes and disappear into the thick woodland at a moment's notice.

After landing and trekking back through the forest they'd seen two ranger's trucks come tearing along one of the wide trails, and seen four rangers fan out through the forest. It was to be expected.

The game of cat and mouse was afoot.

"Yeah, they're gone," Billy said, lowering the high-powered binoculars.

He rose to his feet, gathered up his backpack and changed out of the wingsuit and unscrewed the top of his bottle of water.

"You know, Billy, I was thinking maybe next year we could try Yosemite."

"Yosemite? Why?"

Wyatt threw his hands up. "Are you kidding me? Two words. Taft Point."

He waved him off. "No way, that place is cursed."

"And you think this place is better?"

"At least here we're familiar with the terrain, and we've built a rapport with the rangers."

Wyatt laughed. "Rapport. Oh, we've built a rapport. If they get their hands on us we are looking at some serious jail time."

"If," he said, placing emphasis on the word. "We are always one step ahead."

Wyatt shook his head as they pitched sideways down a steep incline. Billy looked at him and could see he was annoyed.

"What is it?" Billy asked.

"Nothing."

"You're a shitty liar. Come out with it."

"I'm just thinking it's kind of getting old. You know, coming here and doing the whole wild goose chase. We've been lucky so far but I just get a feeling that our luck is about to run out."

Billy chuckled and wrapped his arm around Wyatt's neck. "How long have I known you?"

"Since we were kids."

"And I have ever let you down?"

"No but you've led me into some crazy situations."

"Dude, people sleep their way through life only wishing to be able to do what we do. Look at all the views we've racked up online. You've read the comments. These people think we are gods."

"Idiots, you mean."

Billy brushed past an Engelmann spruce tree.

"Idiots. Gods. At least we are getting paid well. Three years ago we didn't have the sponsors we have now. We were living out of that shitty trailer in Montana, and doing handyman jobs for pennies on the dollar. Did you like that life? No. Now we get to travel all over the USA, dirt-biking, snowboarding, jumping out of planes and soaking in the beauty of God's country. This was the way we were meant to live, Wyatt, not stuck behind a desk as a yes-man. That's not the life for me, and don't you dare say it's what you want as you were the one bellyaching about the shitty jobs we used to do." They made their way over to a clearing, a high precipice that overlooked the lake. "Look at that, Wyatt. Soak it all in. When we are bedridden at the end of our lives you'll remember this, and I guarantee you won't be complaining about causing a little trouble. You'll be laughing your ass off."

"But don't you think there is more to life than this?"

"Like what... Paying taxes? Living paycheck to paycheck? Being someone's bitch? Are you serious?"

He shrugged. "Listen, I like all of this but we're the only ones that benefit."

Billy opened his mouth agape. "Oh, you did not just say that."

"Think about it, Billy."

"I don't need to. We are entertaining the masses. What higher purpose can there be? We pull people out of their dreary lives and for a short while we allow them to imagine they are us. Living the dream. Every person that clicks on one of our videos only wishes they were us. Stop overthinking it."

"It just doesn't feel like we're making a difference."

"What are you, Mother Teresa? You want us to donate

money to the poor? Oh... hold on a minute... you already did. The poor was us. I don't remember anyone giving us shit when we were down and out. Everything we have, we have had to work for. So why the hell I should we give a damn about anyone else?"

Wyatt shook his head. "I'm not talking about donating money. You know what I mean."

"No I don't. So enlighten me."

Wyatt didn't respond so Billy squeezed the back of his neck playfully and he grinned. "Alright, maybe next year we'll check out Yosemite. Sound good?"

Wyatt nodded. "Yeah. Okay."

"Good, now let's head down and get a fire going. I'm starving."

It took them another twenty minutes to work their way down to where the lake was and make their way around to where they'd left their belongings. Billy had camouflaged the dirt bikes with branches from the trees.

"What do you fancy for dinner tonight? Elk or fish?" Billy asked as he uncovered their equipment and brought wood down to the beach so they could start a fire.

"I don't care as long as I don't have to catch it."

"Ah... that's how you want to do this? Fine. You set up the tents and..." He withdrew his Remington 798 rifle and slung it over his shoulder. "I'll see if I can bag us an elk."

"If not, a squirrel will do," Wyatt said in jest.

Billy flipped him the bird and headed into the thick woodland. He'd become a pro at hunting and when he wasn't recording stuff for their channel, he could be found up at his cabin in Montana with his old man fishing and hunting. After some of the extreme sports they did, hunting was the next best thing. He knew there were folks out there who saw it as inhumane or cruel but there was nothing he had killed that hadn't been used up. Excess meat was given to neighbors in his town and the skins went to the local hunting store. He was doing the world a favor.

Billy breathed in the scent of pine and damp soil. He stopped every so often to mark the trees with chalk so he didn't lose his way. As he trudged through the forest he thought about what Wyatt had said. At the age of twenty-four he hadn't really given much weight to future plans. He'd lived his life with the motto that tomorrow may never come, and he squeezed out as much excitement and adventure from each day as humanly possible. A few of his family members said he was a fool to do what he did for a living as the police would one day catch up with him but he didn't believe it. They wore skull and crossbones bandannas over their faces, along with sunglasses. There were no birthmarks or tattoos, nothing that would give them away — unless the cops were good at identifying a person by their voice. And they had an agreement with sponsors to send funds into a PayPal account that he'd paid a close friend to set up. From there they transferred the money out to a bank account as and when they needed it. The account was offshore so they didn't have to worry about the prying eyes of tax people or cops who might see one of their sponsors and try to trace them. So far it had worked.

Billy had been trudging through the forest for what felt like thirty minutes before he came across three elk grazing nearby. He dropped to a knee and breathed slowly as he raised the rifle. "Come to papa," he said, taking his time to get the beauty in the crosshair. He peered through the scope, aiming for a spot one third of the way up the chest to get a double-lung shot. He planned on taking two shots because elk wouldn't always drop right away. Many had run off, and covered more than a hundred yards before they gave up the ghost.

He took a deep breath and let it out slowly as he squeezed the trigger.

The round echoed in the valley.

Sure enough the elk took off, and Billy ended up chasing it and firing off a few more rounds before it dropped. He had no plans of dragging the whole thing out, he only needed enough to last for a few days, and he'd brought with him a tarp, and burlap bags to store the meat, and some rope to drag it out. The rest he would leave for the wolves. Nothing went to waste.

Out of breath from chasing after the beast he finally caught up with it and dropped down, placing his hand on the warm body. With it no longer breathing he went about laying the large tarp and then cutting through the hindquarter. He would debone it to take out some of the weight, and then wrap the rest of the meat in the tarp, leaving behind the bulk of the carcass for nature.

Before beginning he got on the radio to check in with Wyatt and tell him to start a fire. "Wyatt, come in."

"Go ahead."

"Should be back in about half an hour, though it might take me longer as I managed to bag us some elk."

"Take your time. All is good here. No sign of rangers."

Billy withdrew his hunting knife and started carving up the meat. He hadn't been working on it for longer than fifteen minutes when he heard the snap of a branch behind him. Billy whipped around to find a ranger holding a rifle on him. He looked to be in his late twenties. Sharp features, a strong jaw, muscular, someone who obviously wasn't going to be a pushover. His stomach dropped. Why hadn't he heard him creep up?

"You know it's prohibited to hunt in Yellowstone," the ranger said. "You could be looking at six months in jail and a $500 fine."

"It was already dead."

The ranger smirked and his eyes darted around. "Anyone else with you?"

"Just me," Billy said casting a glance to his rifle that was nearby. The ranger caught him looking at it.

"Don't even think about it."

"You law enforcement?"

"What's in the backpack?" the ranger said not answering his question.

"Just a few things needed to survive out here."

"Which campground are you at?"

"I'm not."

"You camping in the backcountry then?"

"Yeah."

"Where?"

Billy was well aware there were 300 designated spots

for backcountry camping, none of which were located in the area he was in. They were positioned closer to the twelve campgrounds.

He lied and said the one he could remember. "Old Faithful."

"You're a long way out. Toss over your backpack."

"No. That's private property."

"So are the elk. Toss it over, and drop that knife while you're at it."

Billy released the knife and got up slowly and walked over to the backpack. It had his wingsuit. "You know I have rights."

"So do the animals," the ranger replied.

"I told you I found it like this."

"Really, then maybe you can explain why I heard a gunshot?"

"I don't know, maybe I scared off the poachers."

"Poachers?"

"Yeah."

"And yet here you are carving up this beautiful

animal."

"Well no point in it going to waste."

He sighed and scooped up the backpack. None of the rangers knew what they looked like because they'd always made a point to wear their bandannas over the lower part of their face in their videos. If it got out who he was, he wouldn't just be facing charges from Yellowstone; there would be multiple parks throughout the USA interested in pressing charges.

Billy stood there staring back. "Look, shouldn't you be showing me some kind of badge?"

The ranger pointed to the patch on his arm. Billy held out the bag.

"Open it."

"Not without a search warrant."

The ranger made a motion with his rifle. "Open it."

"You open it," Billy said tossing it near his feet. The ranger gave him the beady eye before he dropped to a crouch. All the while he kept the rifle on him as he reached for the zipper with the other hand. Billy didn't take his eyes off him. He was waiting for his moment, that split second when the ranger would look down, except it didn't come. He remained focused on him so Billy walked forward.

"Stay where you are."

"Why? It's a free country. I haven't done anything wrong."

"Stay where you are."

He shrugged. "I'm not the one armed."

One thing for sure, he wasn't going in with him. The ranger latched on to the zipper and gave it a tug. He had no other choice but to look down to see inside of it. In that moment, Billy lunged forward knocking the ranger back. The rifle went off and they began wrestling on the ground for control.

He knocked the gun out of his hand and they rolled across the ground, getting covered in dirt, leaves and twigs. The ranger managed to get behind him and tried to put him in a chokehold. Billy began coughing hard and he started to see darkness edging in at the corner of his eyes. If he didn't get loose from his grip immediately it was going to be lights out. As they continued to roll on the ground, he spotted the knife. His hands clawed at the dirt, inching his way toward it.

Darkness closed in.

He was seconds away from passing out when he snagged it up and jammed it as hard as he could into the ranger's leg, then withdrew it. He had no intention of killing him. That wasn't his way but he wasn't going to spend time behind bars.

The ranger screamed in agony and released his grip.

Billy rolled out from under his arm, coughing and spluttering. He took a second before scrambling to his feet and scooping up his rifle. The ranger looked at him with a pained expression, fully expecting him to shoot. Instead, Billy turned and fled.

As he bolted, he heard the ranger shout over the radio.

"Come in control, this is Hayden. I've been stabbed."

Chapter 8

Fear shot through him at the sound of Hayden's cry for help. Logan had been in the process of tracking down Hank when the distress call came over the radio. Hank wasn't answering his phone, and he wasn't making any headway getting a bead on his location in Death Gulch. Logan was the first to respond.

"Hayden, what's your location?"

Static crackled over the radio.

"Just north of Dryad Lake. I've activated the EPIRB so the station should have my position."

"Roger that."

"Logan, it was one of those two assholes. I saw the guy's wingsuit in his backpack. He'd poached an elk. He's around six foot one, wearing jeans, black hiking boots, a green Oakley V-neck T-shirt, and a black North Face windbreaker. He took off heading south towards the lake."

"Got it. How hurt are you?"

"It's bad. My leg's wounded. I've tied it off but I'm bleeding out fast."

"We're coming, buddy. Hang in there."

There were three medical centers in the park, one at Old Faithful, another at Mammoth and the third was at Lake Yellowstone. The staff was more than capable at stabilizing patients through all manner of injuries, though they tended to get far more incidents of chest pain and heart trouble, not stabbings. Depending on the injury, they could arrange a transfer to a nearby hospital.

As soon as Logan finished speaking with Hayden, he called the closest ranger station at Lake Backcountry just south of Fishing Bridge Junction to make sure that they'd picked up the EPIRB distress signal and that the search and rescue helicopter was on its way. Thankfully they were already on it and two rangers were en route. Logan was currently near the Canyon Backcountry Office so it would have taken him a good forty minutes to get close to where Hayden was, and then another forty to hike out.

He figured whoever was responsible for the attack would be long gone by the time the two rangers got down there, however, that didn't mean he would stand by and do nothing. Unable to help the rescue team he headed for the ranger station in Canyon Village to get in contact with the Investigative Services Branch and get their assistance with the apprehension of the two individuals. Among the many facets of protection that Yellowstone provided, the National Park had its own special agents who were on hand when required. As it stood, they needed as much help as they could to find this guy before anyone else got injured.

* * *

Back in Mammoth, Catherine was dealing with her own battle, in the form of her thirteen-year-old son. "I thought we were going to leave?"

"I never said that, Jordan."

"We just experienced an earthquake and you want to stay?"

"Yellowstone has them all the time. I need to speak

with a geologist friend of mine this evening."

"What? We're on vacation. Is this for work?"

"No, it's because of what happened today. Look, I just want to make sure everything is okay. We just arrived here. If things are dangerous, we'll leave. You have my word on that but I have to speak with him first."

Okay so she wasn't exactly telling the truth.

"Your word?"

She nodded. Catherine knew it was risky making a promise. She'd done it before, for his middle school graduation, and once for a track meet — both times she was unable to make it. Though the graduation wasn't her fault. Her flight was cancelled due to bad weather in Chicago.

* * *

A few hours passed and they spent the remainder of the day taking in a few of the local sights like the Boiling River Trail and the Albright Visitor Center, before cooking up some steaks over the fire, and polishing them off with some cheesecake she'd picked up from the hotel.

By the time the sun began to wane behind the trees, Jordan seemed more relaxed. There had only been a couple instances over the afternoon that gave cause for concern, and that was when two ranger SUVs shot by with their lights flashing. She told him that they had to do that even if it wasn't an emergency. It was the only way to cut through the traffic. Strangely he bought it.

Perched on the end of the picnic table, Catherine logged into the University of Utah and checked the seismic data for Yellowstone. The data was off the charts for the brief period that the quake had occurred but then had settled. She glanced over at Jordan and felt a twinge of guilt. It wasn't easy to shut off her mind from work, and even harder after today's incident. After the fissure in Grand Teton National Park and the swarm of earthquakes, Catherine's nerves were on edge. There was only so much they could learn from the seismic, thermal and deformation monitoring, more often than not it required getting boots on the ground and seeing close up what was going on.

"Jordan, do you want to stay here while I'm at this meeting tonight?"

"No, I would prefer to come." He looked around and then returned to flicking through his phone. Catherine hoped he would opt for playing games on his phone, as she didn't want him to be within earshot of the questions she had for Hank.

Unless there was something wrong with the borehole instrumentation at Yellowstone, the increase in seismic activity was disturbing to say the least.

If Hank was concerned, she knew that he would have contacted the USGS. They would have been the first ones to have been alerted. Catherine flipped through her contacts looking for the name. She really didn't want to contact her but she also didn't want to waste her time this evening listening to lies.

Her thumb hovered over the name, Rebecca Lyons.

Chapter 9

Answers. Logan wanted answers and he'd been told by Hank he'd get them at the meeting that night. It was to be held at the park headquarters in Mammoth Hot Springs at seven o'clock. It had been the second time in his career that he'd been called in to an official meeting with the superintendent; the last time was back in August of 2013 when the Alum Fire ripped through 7,500 acres. What a joke that was. Meetings turned into arguments as forest supervisors and park officials wrestled with the monumental task before them. Hundreds of firefighters from as far as Hawaii and Florida had been flown in to help, followed by the military. That event had been a prime example of how unprepared they were for evacuating visitors. They had to ride horses into the backcountry to alert them to the approaching fire.

A blanket of acrid smoke had smothered the park and its gateway communities as troops of military personnel joined firefighters and helicopters dumped water. It was a disorganized mess and looked more like a war zone than the flourishing park that attracted millions each year. Back then they were fighting a natural fire, and even with over 9,500 firefighters and 115 aircraft, they still had a hard time stopping the fire and smoke from spreading. It had swept across thousands of acres in a matter of days, and Logan had seen the 200-foot flames force out the remaining tourists. Many of the backcountry fires that weren't a threat to buildings were allowed to run their course while experienced firefighters put all their efforts into stopping the larger fires and protecting surrounding communities. Backfires were lit. Tourism was affected. Residents were angry, and thousands of firefighters were fatigued. Six days into September and over one million acres still raged out of control. If it wasn't for the rain that arrived on the eleventh day of that month, they might have lost the entire park, and most of the surrounding communities. That's what worried him now. If Yellowstone erupted nothing would stop it. Not rain. Not the government. No feat of engineering. And it wouldn't spread slowly either. If it unzipped the way most expected, thousands within 500 miles of the park would die instantly. And it wouldn't stop there. Scalding hot ash would move beyond that at hurricane speeds, breaking trees like matchsticks, killing people, plants and animals and crushing buildings. Even a few inches of ash would have the potential to shut down air travel, destroy farms, clog roadways, cause respiratory problems, block sewer lines and short out transformers.

With all this in mind, he'd already had that conversation with the park geologist and his reply was clear — the only recourse would be to get as far away as possible.

Easy to say if someone was already out of the hot zone, harder for those in Wyoming, Montana, Idaho, Utah, Colorado, South Dakota and further afield.

When Logan arrived that evening, he surveyed the concerned faces in the room. In attendance were Chief McDonald; the superintendent of the park, William

Harris; geologist Hank Peters; Holly Reed, the head of concessions management; two employees who oversaw strategic communications; and Philip Weston, another park ranger.

Hank was already in a heated discussion with Chief McDonald, and Harris was trying to intervene. Logan couldn't tell what it was about but he was fairly confident that McDonald felt his manhood was being threatened. The guy didn't budge an inch when it came to being told what to do.

Harris threw a hand up, and pulled at his own tie with the other. "Calm down. Calm down. Let's not lose our focus here."

William Harris was a small, ginger haired, overweight man who looked as if he was one cheeseburger away from a heart attack. He braced himself against the boardroom table and wiped sweat from his brow with a handkerchief. His cheeks were flush as though he'd just stepped off a treadmill.

"As I was saying before I was rudely cut off," Hank

glared at McDonald, "I think we should contact the USGS to have them come down and assist us based on today's events and my findings."

"Did those findings include the road melting?" Logan asked stepping into the room. All eyes turned on him. McDonald was quick to question what he was doing there. Logan answered, "I was invited, and quite frankly even if I wasn't I'd still be here. I warned you eight months ago about the possibility of the caldera spreading but you wouldn't listen."

"Oh, please, stop!" McDonald said. "Listen, we sympathize with the loss of your fiancée, Logan, and we are deeply sorry that accident happened but that was ruled a—"

"I know what it was ruled but that doesn't explain how it happened, and neither does it explain why the road over by Fire Hole is now melting."

"I already told you. The roadwork was given to the lowest bidder. There is nothing mysterious about it."

"No? What about animals fleeing the park in large

numbers, or better still, why did an entire lake of fish die today? Huh? Should we blame that on the lowest bidder?"

He stared back at them and they looked at Hank. Logan's eyes darted between them.

"What is it?" Logan asked, getting the feeling that they knew something he didn't.

Hank, a wiry man in his mid-thirties with a balding head, cleared his throat, adjusted his thick-rimmed spectacles and stepped away from a table he was perched on. "I found two grizzlies and their cubs dead over in Death Gulch today."

"And it just gets better. How many times do we have to go over this?" McDonald said. "Bears die all the time in this park and until an autopsy can be done on those, we are dealing with nothing more than speculation."

"Speculation? The CO_2 and H_2S readings were extremely high."

"For that area. For that time. You said yourself that the park is releasing gases all over the place. One area it might be concentrated, and in another it might be fine. The only way to determine if that spot is dangerous is to monitor it over time."

"And the quake?" Hank asked.

"The same."

"Dear God, man, how can you be so blind?" Logan said. "We haven't experienced a quake on the level of what we had today."

"We experience them all the time, and you know it," McDonald said. "You just want to make this about what happened to Jenna." Logan moved in closer, his eyes narrowed. He'd always been cautious of what he said around McDonald because he was his superior but he could feel himself losing his cool. The chief continued, "Every year, we experience upwards of a thousand to three thousand earthquakes, some of those are of a magnitude of 3 and 4, and some of those are felt by people in the park. In all this time has Yellowstone erupted? No. And I don't expect it to. Both of you are acting paranoid and quite frankly it needs to stop." Chief McDonald turned to Harris. "Sir—"

"What you call paranoia, we call data, and it can save lives," a female said from behind them. Logan turned to see an attractive woman with long dark hair enter the room. She had an oval face, large eyes and an athletic appearance. She was wearing jeans, a cream-colored shirt and brown boots. Behind her, just beyond the door was a teenage boy glancing down at his phone. She turned and muttered something to him and he walked off down the hall, no longer in sight.

McDonald's brow furrowed. "Who are you?"

Before she could reply, Hank stepped forward.

"Catherine. Glad you could make it," Hank said strolling over and giving her a hug. "Everyone, this is Catherine Shaw from the University of Utah. She's one of the analysts, and a former volcanologist for the USGS."

"Oh great, should we expect the media next?" McDonald said lifting his arms in the arm and slumping into a chair before shaking his head.

"Hank, did you contact the university about this?" Harris asked, a look of concern spreading over his face.

He shook his head. "No. I haven't been in contact with anyone besides Catherine and yourselves. I was planning on speaking with USGS after this meeting."

"No need, I already have," Catherine said. "I talked to Rebecca this evening. They were already on route. It seems that quake was an M5.9 and along with other abnormal seismic changes, it concerned them enough to board a plane for here."

McDonald put his head in his hands.

"Did you take gas samples when you were in Death Gulch?" Catherine asked.

"You heard about that?" Hank replied.

"And other things," she said glancing at Logan and then McDonald.

Hank nodded. "The COSPEC readings were high."

"Just as I thought. Look, what can you tell me about NASA's work here in the park?"

"How do you know about that?" Harris asked.

"Why wouldn't she?" Logan asked. "It's been common knowledge for some time. Hell, *National Geographic* even ran an article about it. It's Internet fodder. Though I'd be interested in knowing why our department wasn't informed about their presence in the park."

"I'm afraid that's above your pay grade," Harris said.

"When it's my life at stake, and the lives of thousands of visitors, I would beg to differ."

Harris sighed and ran a hand over his head. "Well then let's get something out of the way immediately. What is discussed here today remains between us. As you are aware, the magma is only a threat if it is molten. To decrease the danger of an eruption, the drill is not going to pierce the magma chamber as that obviously has the potential to cause an eruption. It will be burrowing ten kilometers into the hydrothermal fluids around the chamber in order to draw away heat. This will chill anything that is molten and eradicate the potential of an eruption."

"I thought that project had been abandoned?" Philip asked. "I heard the logistics of getting water, and burrowing that deep into the earth, was too great."

Harris replied, "Delayed. Yes. Abandoned. No. The project has been in the works for several years now; they just haven't been able to determine the best way to approach it until now. They are confident that it can be done, and in light of the increased earthquake swarm activity, we don't exactly have a choice."

"So that's what caused the quake today?" Philip asked.

Harris turned to him again. "From my discussions with NASA, yes."

"And the dead bears, the fish, the melting road?" Logan asked.

"That was news to me."

Catherine frowned. "The initial magma chamber is anywhere from three to nine miles below the surface. Historically we haven't burrowed deeper than 7.1 miles."

"Exactly," Philip said. "So are you telling me they now have the technology to do this? And how can they be sure they aren't burrowing into the magma? I thought the seismic monitors only check a few miles below the surface?"

"There is still much about the caldera that we don't know," Hank said.

"I second that. Like, the possibility that it's bigger than we once thought, or that it's moved closer to the surface," Logan said.

"We are not here to speculate," Harris said.

"Hear, hear!" McDonald added.

"It's not speculation," Catherine chimed in. "Three years ago we took images of a reservoir of hot, partly molten rock, twelve to twenty-eight miles below the super volcano. It's 4.4 times larger than the shallow magma chamber that you all know about. Essentially there is enough molten rock in there to fill the Grand Canyon 11.2 times, while the magma chamber you all know about would fill it 2.5 times." She paused to let that sink in.

"Well that certainly puts things in perspective," Logan said. "And in light of this I think it makes sense to at least make the tourists aware that we might be looking at evacuating them."

"Hold on a minute," McDonald said rising to his feet.

"Let's not jump the gun here. You saw what happened back in 2013. I think we need to be very careful about the decisions we make. There are over 9,000 visitors this month in the park."

"And that's why we should get ahead of this while we can," Logan said.

McDonald jabbed his finger at Logan. "You are overstepping the line."

"And you're underestimating the threat."

"I think he has a point, Chief," Philip said. "Someone lost their life out on that lake today."

Things were starting to get heated so Harris stepped forward.

"Settle down. The reason I called this meeting was to inform you of the work that NASA is doing, not to start an argument." He turned to Logan. "Look, what's the update on Hayden?"

Logan sighed and ran a hand over his head. "He's been taken to Lake Clinic with a stab wound to the leg. He was very lucky that SAR reached him in time. I was planning on going down to see him in the morning."

"And the man who did it?"

"ISB has been alerted, and law enforcement rangers have an APB out on the guy. We don't have a description of the second man and there is a possibility that they aren't traveling together."

McDonald walked over to one of the windows and looked out into the darkness. "Chances of us finding him tonight are slim to none." He shook his head. "We should have had these guys two years ago." He cast a glance Logan's way as if all the responsibility fell on his shoulders. The fact was they had done everything they could to apprehend the individuals but they were slippery and as familiar with the park as any ranger. They even thought that there was a possibility that it was a disgruntled ranger, though that idea was quickly shot down by McDonald.

"You mentioned that USGS are on the way. Did they say when they would get here?" Harris asked Catherine.

"Either late tonight or by morning."

Harris nodded. "Okay, well until then I don't want what we have discussed to go any further. That means if the media come knocking, no one else is to know about today's events until we can figure out what's happening." Harris looked exasperated as he shook his head and left the room with McDonald in his shadow. Hank went over to Catherine and started chatting with her as Logan went to leave the room.

"Oh Logan, you mind if I have a word?" Hank said. He nodded and came back over to where both of them were. "I'm sorry for not informing you about NASA's presence. Harris had me under a strict no-tell policy."

"I understand." He glanced at Catherine and she smiled back.

"That your boy out there?" Logan asked gesturing with his head to the kid who was parked outside the front door in a chair.

"Yep." She stared out absently. "I mean he resembles my boy, though lately he hasn't been acting like the one I once knew." She turned back to him. "I was hoping this trip would give us time to bond again. Boy, was I wrong."

His eyes dropped to her hand where he noticed she wasn't wearing a wedding ring.

"I think we could all use a drink. I was going to show Catherine some of the data and readings I've collected over the past few months, would you care to join us?"

Logan cast a glance over his shoulder, and sucked air between his teeth.

"Ah, why not. In theory my shift finished an hour ago."

Chapter 10

The dirt bikes wailed, spitting dirt in every direction as Billy and Wyatt zigzagged their way west through the dark, gloomy forest. He hadn't told Wyatt that he'd stabbed a ranger and despite his best effort to conceal his panic, Wyatt knew something was wrong. Hours earlier, upon sprinting back to the lake, Billy had told Wyatt to leave the tents, and to take nothing more than his rifle and backpack. He uncovered the dirt bikes and they took off heading south in an attempt to escape the park. All the while Wyatt kept pestering him with questions. "What's going on? Where are we going? Billy, slow down." But he wouldn't slow until he was far away from the park. This was the last time he would ever step foot inside its boundaries. The last time he would enter any national park and taunt rangers. It wasn't meant to go this way. If the damn ranger had just let him go… why didn't he let him go? They were just trying to have some fun. They hadn't hurt anyone… until now.

As the bikes shot past trees, over rocky rises, and down steep inclines Billy thought about the look on that ranger's face. He couldn't get his face out of his mind. Was he alive? Dead? Had he killed him? The thought horrified him.

Wyatt came alongside him and tried to flag him down for the fourth time but he wasn't paying attention. They didn't have the luxury of time. By now the park would be full of law enforcement looking for them. That six months in jail and $500 fine for poaching would be nothing compared to what he would get if they got hold of him.

Eager to get him to stop and unable to get him to listen, Wyatt gave him a shove with his foot. Billy's bike wobbled, and his eyes widened as he barreled towards a tree. He turned at the last second, skidding across the ground, and wiped out hard.

Wyatt came to a halt a few feet from him, took off his helmet and shut off his bike. He scrambled over to make sure he was okay. Furious, panic stricken, and not thinking straight, Billy lashed out with a right hook and clocked him on the jaw, knocking him back.

Wyatt rubbed his jaw as he looked up at him. "What the fuck?"

Billy got up and headed over to his bike but the front wheel was busted up, and there was a huge amount of dirt in the engine. "Shit!" He slammed the bike back down and clenched his fist, casting a sideways glare at Wyatt. "Why the hell did you do that?"

"You wouldn't listen," Wyatt said. "One minute you are all cheery on the radio because you've bagged an elk, the next you're hurrying back telling me to leave the tents. What's going on? What happened?"

Billy placed his hands on his knees trying to catch his breath. He looked around trying to get a bearing on where they were. At night every direction inside Yellowstone's forest looked the same. A crescent moon shone down, rays of light breaking through the canopy of leaves.

"Billy. What's up?"

"Shut up." He listened intently, trying to filter out the noise of the forest and listen for the sound of horses or helicopters. There was no way they could get a truck this far into the forest but he knew they would be out searching for them. Earlier that afternoon they'd heard a helicopter. He wasn't sure if it was for them or for the ranger and he didn't stick around to find out.

Fear dominated. He wasn't one to lose his cool. It was the reason why they had racked up such a strong following of fans that tuned into to see their exploits, but tackling law enforcement — that was another thing entirely.

"If you're worried about the rangers, don't be. They haven't seen our faces," Wyatt said.

He looked over to him, fine lines forming on his brow.

"Billy?" There was a pause. "They haven't seen our faces. Right?"

When Billy didn't immediately give him an answer, Wyatt slammed a fist into the earth. "Shit. Shit! Shit!" He got up and paced back and forth. "So they saw you? Is that it?"

"He came out of nowhere. I didn't hear him until he was on me."

"Alright but you got away. So why all the panic? It's just a ranger. It's not like the first time we've been confronted by one."

Billy's chin dropped.

"Billy."

"He was going to turn us in. We would have got time."

"Billy."

"I didn't have much choice. He had a gun on me. He wanted to look in the backpack. He would have seen the wingsuit. We would have been exposed."

Wyatt walked over to him and grabbed him by the shoulders. "What did you do?"

"I was going to run…" he stumbled over his words. "But I saw the knife and…"

Wyatt stared at him in disbelief. "Did you kill him?"

"I don't know. I was just trying to keep him back. I thought he would back off but he wouldn't. We started struggling. His gun went off and the next thing I knew I had the knife in my hand and..." He stopped as memories of it flashed back and he felt like throwing up. He leaned to one side and coughed and gagged. As he wiped his mouth, dried blood smeared across his lips. Was it the elk's or the ranger's blood? He felt his gag reflex kick in again.

Wyatt staggered back and leaned against a tree. "I knew it. I knew one of these days things would go south." He kept shaking his head and looking off into the darkness. "I told you we should have left. We could have been gone by now. No one would have been the wiser but no, you insisted on staying."

Billy looked over at him from his position on the forest floor. His hands were covered in grime. He could see Wyatt was teetering on the edge of a dark abyss, looking into a space he might not come back from. Billy rose from the ground and stumbled over to him. He placed a hand on Wyatt's shoulder. "Listen…"

Wyatt shook it off. "No. I've listened enough to you and where's it got us?" Silence stretched between them, then Wyatt spoke again, "Hold on a minute. They're out there looking for you. Not me."

"What?"

"Yeah, you stabbed him. Not me. They don't know what I look like."

Billy studied his friend's face.

"I can leave. I can go. If I'm stopped the ranger won't identify me."

"No. You're in this as deep as I am. They find that wingsuit on you and…"

Before he could finish what he was saying, Wyatt removed his backpack and unzipped it. He yanked out the suit and tossed it into the darkness. "You were saying?"

Without another word he put the backpack on and mounted his dirt bike, getting ready to ride out. Billy hurried over to him and placed both hands on the handles.

"You gonna leave me out here?"

"Well you were going to drag me into this."

"Get off the bike, Wyatt."

Wyatt ignored him and slipped on his helmet. He mumbled the word no, and tried to kick-start it to life. Billy shoved him, making him lose his balance and fall to one side. Wyatt braced himself with one foot and tried to straighten up but Billy prevented him.

"Get off, Billy."

"How many times did I help you out? Who gave you a room after your old man turfed you out? Who paid for food when you didn't have a job? Huh?"

Wyatt stared back, nothing more than his eyes visible.

"I messed up," Billy said. "I can't change that."

"I'm not going down for your mistake. It's one thing to help a friend in need, another to drag him down with you. You expect me to do hard time for you?"

"No. I didn't say that."

"And yet by staying with you, I will be guilty by

association."

Billy stared at him, holding the bike there for a minute or two until he released the handlebars. Without saying another word he walked a short distance away and slumped down in front of a tree. Wyatt didn't waste a minute. He fired up the engine, flipped down his goggles, gave one final glance at Billy and then tore off into the night.

Chapter 11

The atmosphere inside Mammoth Hot Springs Hotel was eerily calm despite experiencing such a strong earthquake earlier that day. As neither of them had eaten dinner, Hank suggested they get a table in the newly renovated historic building. Hank, a history buff who nearly went into archeology before he became a geologist, was more than eager to give Catherine the background on Yellowstone's first hotel that had opened back in 1883.

Crowded around a small table, Hank spent the better part of the meal showing Catherine the data while Logan spoke with Jordan about his love of basketball. It had been the first time since they'd arrived that she'd seen a smile on his face. Richard had never been a big sports fan, even though he had taken Jordan to games over the years.

Hank leaned back in his seat, and wiped the corners of his lips.

The smell and sizzle of steak dominated as a waiter

came out and delivered the juicy dish to one of the guests across from them. They themselves had opted for pasta. Catherine and Hank had a couple of beers to ease their nerves.

"Yeah, so they finished off turning the map room into this lounge back in late December. The gift shop was extended, and the second floor offices are now used for public meetings. I think they've done a good job." Catherine gazed at the large wooden wall map that was created by the architect Robert Reamer back in the 1930s. They'd just got it back from a restoration at the NPS conservation lab in Arizona so Hank was proud to show it off.

"I like it," she said.

It was cozy. Waiters in crisp black-and-white uniforms moved quickly around tables serving patrons. The sound of clinking glass and cutlery was barely noticeable over chatter.

"They're planning on closing it down this winter because they want to remodel the 30-plus rooms, as they don't have any bathrooms, and they will be updating it all."

"Let's hope it survives long enough for us to see it," Logan said leaning forward.

Catherine took a sip of her drink. "Is he always like that. The chief?"

"Only when he doesn't take his bipolar medication."

Hank nearly spat out beer. He burst into laughter.

"Don't let him catch you saying that."

"Ah, he already knows I don't like him," Logan said.

"You don't get along?" Catherine asked.

"No, we haven't seen eye to eye since Je…" he trailed off and Catherine noticed his head drop a little.

"She was your girlfriend?"

"Was. Yeah."

There was a pause.

"Do you mind me asking what happened?"

He cleared his throat and looked at her as if he wasn't sure.

"You don't have to."

"No, it's okay." Logan glanced at Hank. "Eight months ago we were out at Shoshone Canyon. Myself, Jenna, and two friends."

"Hayden," Hank interjected. "Another ranger."

Logan nodded.

"She went into the river with Allison and…" he trailed off and got this faraway look in his eye as if he was reliving it again. "The water began to boil. I tried to get to her but it was too hot." He breathed in deeply. "She went under and her body was recovered a day later downstream."

"I'm sorry."

"So am I." He took a hard pull on his glass of whiskey. "Anyway, they ruled it an accident. The result of a phenomenon. Isn't that what they called it, Hank?"

Hank looked bothered. He nodded.

"But you think it was related to the caldera?"

"It doesn't matter what I think. As long as the powers that be are calling the shots, as long as this park is full, and the surrounding towns are busy, that's all that matters. Keep the machine going. Isn't that right, Hank?"

Hank nodded, then finished off his drink. He cleared his throat. "Well, I should really turn in for the night. I hope you two don't mind but I have a big day ahead and I have a feeling the superintendent is going to drag me back into another meeting tomorrow." He rolled his eyes.

"Oh by all means," Catherine said.

"Catherine, it was lovely to see you again. And you too, Jordan."

Hank cracked a smile.

"Logan."

"Hank," he replied.

Hank gathered up his laptop and rolls of paper full of seismic data he'd brought with him and headed out leaving them alone. Catherine looked over at Jordan and ran a hand through his hair. He shook her hand off and Logan noticed.

"You know I was like that when I was a kid. I mean, not with my head in a phone. But I didn't see the value of a place like this."

She frowned. "So what changed?"

"A trip with my father. My parents were divorced and he was big on the outdoors. I guess he wanted to impart some of that before he passed away."

"He's gone?"

"Died of cancer, a year after that camping trip." Logan shook his head ever so slowly. "I guess it stuck with me. Made me think about what was really important. Up until that point I had my eyes set on living in the big city. New York, that is. I was going to go into advertising. Can you imagine that?"

"Quite the career choice."

"Yeah. Thankfully, I pursued a career as a ranger and despite the headaches of dealing with an old-timer like McDonald, I wouldn't want to do anything else."

"Even though it puts you in the bull's-eye?"

He chuckled. "Yeah, you'd think I'd be smart and take a position at one of the national parks out east. In fact Jenna's father wanted me to go there." His eyes glazed over and she could sense his loss. Logan took another hard pull on his drink. "So you really think this is the one?"

Her eyebrows rose. "Oh, that Yellowstone is going to erupt?"

He nodded.

"If I hadn't heard of NASA trying to play god, no. I'm used to crunching numbers, Logan. Basically I analyze eruptions, tremors and all manner of strange things that would give most people cause for alarm but that's because they're not familiar with volcanic behavior. Every volcano is different and it can take years of studying them to understand the patterns of behavior, and that's why it's important that we don't misinterpret the data."

He leaned back in his seat, and turned his glass slowly. "So do you think we are misinterpreting data?"

"I think we need to be sure before we raise the alarm."

"Because it would be damaging, raise trust issues and destroy business in towns," a female voice said from behind her. "I'm glad to see you have learned."

Catherine swiveled in her seat to find the research

geophysicist, otherwise known online as the scientist-in-charge of the Yellowstone Volcano Observatory.

Catherine groaned inwardly. She detested the woman. "Logan, this is Rebecca Lyons. She works for the YVO, and was at one time a colleague of mine."

"Your boss, you mean."

"Boss. Colleague. Whatever," Catherine said.

Rebecca smirked as she picked up her glass of wine from the bar and walked over. Beside her was a team of four. Catherine recognized a couple of the faces but there were a couple she hadn't met. They greeted her warmly unlike Rebecca who took a seat without asking if she could join them.

"I hope she hasn't filled your head with too many horror stories, ranger…" she fished for his name.

"Logan Miller. A pleasure."

She extended a hand and eyed him like she was sizing up her next sexual achievement.

"The pleasure is mine." She turned her attention to Jordan at the end of the table. "Jordan? Wow, you've grown up. You're the spitting image of your father. The last time I saw you I was…"

"… climbing out of my bed?" Catherine said. The memory of finding her and Richard together came back like a bad nightmare.

Jordan's eyes darted between them as Rebecca smiled. "You're not still sore over that, are you?"

"Oh no. I've moved on. And from what I recall I believe he did the same with you." Catherine smiled, taking another sip of her drink.

A scowl formed on Rebecca's face. Humiliation. It probably wasn't the best thing to say but it had to be said. She didn't expect Rebecca to be any less lenient with her but at least she could beat her to the punch with an insult.

"I spoke to Hank on the way in. He told me about the meeting you had with the superintendent. I'm glad to see you showed restraint this time around."

"Excuse me?" Catherine said.

Rebecca took a sip of her drink and turned to Logan.

"Did she tell you about Mammoth Lakes? Not Mammoth in Yellowstone, I'm referring to the one in California."

Catherine's jaw tightened. Logan looked at her, slightly confused.

"No? Strange. Oh I would have thought that you would have told them about that. Especially since the town of Mammoth Lakes sits on the Long Valley Caldera."

"Drop it, Rebecca."

She ignored her and continued. "Back when she was working for the USGS. The town experienced six M6 earthquakes. They were monitoring at the time and discovered that the lava dome had risen by... what was it, five or ten inches?"

Catherine gritted her teeth. She had a good mind to toss her drink on her but with Jordan sitting there she didn't want to cause a scene.

"Anyway, there were many more earthquakes and the dome continued to rise. At this point, Catherine issued a notice of a potential volcanic hazard. This occurred just before a local weekend festival. You can imagine what impact it had." She let her words linger. "That's right, the tourists stayed at home. Not long after this the economy went through a slump, housing prices dropped and over the next few years businesses closed, shopping centers were empty and most of the community decided to look for jobs and housing elsewhere. A year later two M5 earthquakes, and another swarm of smaller earthquakes hit the town. There was also more ground deformation and once again Catherine wanted to place the town on high alert in preparation for a disaster. Thankfully that's when I came into the picture and prevented it from happening. The third time. Yes, there was a third time three years later. Who wanted to issue a warning alert?" She winked and Catherine gripped her glass tightly as Rebecca stared back at her. "However, thankfully the caldera didn't erupt. You see, even though they have had many earthquakes and the dome has risen, there has been no eruption. Well, there hasn't been an eruption for over 700,000 years."

"How many inches would give you cause for alarm?" Logan asked.

"Well let's put it this way… a caldera near Naples, Italy rose up nine feet and it didn't erupt, another one in Papua New Guinea rose by more than six feet and nothing happened. Which I might add could explain the flooding that you had today with the lake and the dead fish. Again, it's not good news but it doesn't mean it's going to erupt." She took a sip of her drink. "The truth is, Logan, places like Yellowstone and Long Valley might produce volcanic eruptions that squeeze out magma from time to time but it's liable to come out like toothpaste, not as an explosion."

"Or it can blow up and kill thousands," Catherine added. "Let's not forget that scenario."

"Unlikely," Rebecca added. "Most of the material under Yellowstone is not molten, it's hot, plastic-like rock. The upper magma chamber has around 9 percent molten rock, and the lower chamber about 2 percent."

"That's an estimation. It's not exact science."

"I believe that data came from the University of Utah, not us," Rebecca said glibly and in a manner that made Catherine feel like they were playing a game. A glint in Rebecca's eye obviously indicated she thought she was winning.

"Well with your expertise I'm sure you'll have no problem calming the fears of officials here then," Catherine said. "That is, if your data is correct."

"We haven't been wrong so far."

"So far," Catherine added. "There is always a first. Let's hope people don't lose their lives here. You see, Rebecca, I might have issued a warning too soon in Mammoth Lakes but if push came to shove, and I had to make that call again, I wouldn't change one damn thing. I would rather be wrong and see lives saved than wrong and have thousands of deaths on my conscience."

Rebecca snorted. "Richard said you were like this."

"Like?"

She sniffed and glanced around the room as if she owned it or thought she was better than others. Instead of finishing what she was saying she changed the subject knowing it would piss Catherine off even more. And it did.

"So Logan, do you live north of the park?"

Catherine narrowed her eyes and glared at her.

Logan must have picked up on it as he answered her without giving further details. "Yeah. Tell me, Miss Lyons, what happens if you are wrong?"

"Excuse me?"

"Well, I mean, like Catherine said, there is always a first time." He gave a thin smile and Catherine returned the same.

"It's possible but unlikely while I'm at the helm."

Logan chuckled. "I applaud your confidence but confidence has been proven to get people killed in this park. Actually last week a woman was gored. Strangest thing she said as she was airlifted out of here. She said she didn't think the bison would do anything. Can you believe that?"

Catherine had to stifle a laugh. She wasn't laughing at

the woman's demise but at the point he was making. Rebecca was cocky. She'd become lax in her position and took every opportunity to blow her own horn. The same confidence was liable to get thousands killed if she wasn't careful.

"I guess what I'm trying to say is that when it comes to Mother Nature, sometimes it's better to err on the side of caution. I would rather get it wrong and deal with the backlash of my peers than do nothing and have to face the families of the deceased."

Rebecca snorted and smiled at her team. "Well, we are professionals, Mr. Miller. We get it right so you and others don't have to deal with the consequences of amateur mistakes." She glanced at Catherine.

Catherine had just about enough of her pious attitude. It hadn't changed in all the years she'd known her. She had forgotten what a bitch she could be, and how much she appreciated no longer working for the USGS. She tossed her napkin down. "Jordan. Let's go."

Rebecca's eyes widened. "Leaving so soon? No time for

a drink with an old friend?"

"Excuse us, Logan." She smiled and took a hold of Jordan's arm and motioned for him to leave. With that said they turned and exited the lounge leaving her to gloat about her achievements in the USGS.

Chapter 12

The roar of an engine woke Billy from his slumber. Billy glanced at his watch; it was a little after seven. A bright morning sun filtered through the canopy of trees breathing life to the forest floor. The chirping of birds was a welcome sound after a jumpy night. Every time he heard a sound he would check to see if it was a bear or rangers. He pawed at his weary eyes as the world around him came back into view. The temperature had dropped that night, making it even harder to sleep, and with little to keep him warm except a pit fire, the constant threat of being caught, and an uncomfortable backpack as a cushion, he was lucky to have got five hours' sleep.

He regretted leaving some of their belongings in the tents back at the lake.

Panic set in at the thought of rangers moving in on him, but those fears soon disappeared when Wyatt came into view, tearing up the slope. He sat up and pressed his back against a tree and watched as he rolled into the camp, and shut off the engine. Wyatt flipped up his goggles and looked at him. Neither of them said anything. Wyatt removed his helmet and leaned on his handlebars. "You sleep against that tree all night?"

"Most of it."

Wyatt hauled off his backpack and tossed it over to him. As it hit the ground, several cans of beans, and peaches rolled out.

"Thought you might be hungry."

Billy snagged up one of the cans and looked at it before glancing at him. "You came back. Why?"

Wyatt sniffed hard and surveyed the area. "I got thinking about what you said last night. I drove for hours, and eventually made it over to West Yellowstone. I could have kept on going and headed home but…" he trailed off. "What kind of friend would I be if I did that?"

Billy's face curved into a smile, as Wyatt dismounted his bike.

"Anyway, I stopped at Madison Campground on the

way back and stole a few cans from an RV. Let me tell you, Billy, there is a strong law enforcement presence on the main roads. They're stopping vehicles and handing out flyers. Someone threw one out of their window and I scooped it up. Take a look." He reached into his jacket and pulled out a piece of folded yellow paper and handed it to Billy. Billy opened it to find information on himself. There was no photo but they had his description down to a tee.

"There's a change of clothes in the backpack. I stole those too. Thought you might need them."

Wyatt then scooped up some dry branches and tossed them on the fire to bring it back to life. It had died down overnight and was barely alight. Nothing more than golden embers flickered. Getting down on his hands and knees, Wyatt blew into the fire, smoke circled up and the dying embers came to life. He coughed a few times before backing away. "Fortunately I wasn't stopped. I kept to the trails but it's bad out there. They are serious about finding you."

"No reward for my capture?" Billy chuckled until Wyatt gave him a serious look.

Billy scrunched up the paper and tossed it into the fire. "Well, let's have breakfast and get the hell out of here."

"Yeah about that," he said turning towards his bike. "I'm nearly out of gas."

"So we head down to the marina on Yellowstone Lake. I'm sure we can siphon some from one of the trucks in Bridge Bay Campground."

"Oh yeah, why don't we just fire off a flare while we are at it? Are you serious!? You should have seen Madison Campground. The place was swarming with rangers. I was lucky to not get stopped. They'll have all the major campgrounds on high alert. And as for this morning… they are going to be out in full force searching these forests for us."

"Us? Yesterday it was me," Billy said changing into the new set of clothes.

Wyatt blew out his cheeks and ran a hand around his neck. "That was then, this is now."

Billy finished putting on a black sweater and a warm red jacket before stretching his limbs. Every muscle in his body ached. The hard ground was unforgiving, as was the cold night. It felt like his joints had seized up. He groaned and yawned again. "Well for what it's worth, I appreciate you coming back, Wyatt."

He extended a hand and Wyatt clasped it and they hugged it out.

Over the next half an hour they cooked up the beans they had and downed the peaches. It felt good to get some grub in him. They rehashed the events of the day before Billy apologized for not telling him sooner and for acting as if Wyatt owed him anything.

"Once we have some gas, we'll head east to Cody and then head north into Montana. If we make it back to Harlowton, we'll keep our heads down for a couple of months and things should blow over," Billy said, reaching for a cigarette and then lighting it.

"Or we could head out east. To Maine."

"You still haven't given up on that, have you?"

"My uncle says the wages are good out there as a fisherman. He told me he would hire us. We'd probably earn more than we do now."

"We make a good living from sponsors."

"It's been dwindling, Billy, and you know it. The whole online video gig has changed over the past year."

He nodded. Wyatt was right. Advertisers only paid the big bucks to guys who were doing bigger and better things and while they had cornered the market on crazy antics in national parks, it was becoming old. There were more eyeballs on the athletes sponsored by Red Bull, and they were no athletes, just guys with a taste for the extreme. "All right."

"All right?" Wyatt asked in a surprised manner.

"Yeah. You want to head out east we'll do that."

"Are you serious?"

Billy smiled. "Yes, Wyatt. Now drop it before I change my mind."

Wyatt got all excited and started going on about all the opportunities that were available in Maine, and how the women were much better there—something to do with all that fresh coastal air. It was bullshit but Billy played along with it, if only to keep Wyatt happy. Right now all he wanted was to get the hell out of the park as soon as possible and if agreeing to some asinine road trip out east was what would get him there, then he was game.

* * *

Catherine had got up early that morning to pack the tent and camping gear. Their spot down at Bridge Bay Campground was already reserved for the rest of the week, and she wanted to get a head start on the day. Hank had wanted her to head over to Death Gulch to see for herself and she wanted to, but on the other hand she needed to spend time with Jordan. He wasn't happy about staying and after the previous day, he'd phoned his dad. Richard had wanted to speak with her but she was in no mood so she expected a call today.

"I don't understand why we have to go to the lake. Isn't that where all the dead fish are?"

"You heard that?" Catherine asked.

"Of course, I was outside the room."

"What else did you hear?"

"Something about NASA drilling. Bears that are dead. And not telling anyone else."

Catherine groaned inwardly as she cleaned off the breakfast plates in a bowl of water, and handed them to Jordan to dry. "We'll find out today what is going on and…"

Jordan's phone rang and he answered it.

"Oh hey dad." He paused. "Yeah, she's here."

Right on time, Catherine thought. She glanced at her watch. It was a little after eight which meant it was even earlier where he was. Jordan handed over his phone and she braced herself for the onslaught of questions.

"Hello Richard."

"Don't hello me. Why did you dodge my phone call last night?"

"I was tired. I'd had one hell of a day and…"

"So are you leaving this morning?"

"For Bridge Bay Campground, yes."

"No, I meant the park. I want Jordan on a flight back to California today."

"Then you are out of luck as it's not happening."

"Do I need to get the courts involved? You remember what happened the last time I did that."

"You know, Richard, I'm getting a little tired of your threats. You want to call the courts, and turn this whole thing into a tug of war, be my guest, otherwise back the hell off. I have as much right to parent our kid as you do."

"Yeah, except that involves actually parenting."

Catherine hung up on him. She was seething. The nerve of the man. The phone rang again but she ignored it. Jordan went to take it and she told him to leave it. "Finish drying up and helping me pack up the SUV."

"Are we leaving?" Jordan asked.

"No!" she snapped. "We are going to have a good time for a week if it kills me."

Jordan stared back at her, a look of shock on his face. He returned to drying a pot and she felt a twinge of guilt.

She exhaled hard and then apologized. "Jordan, I'm sorry. I'm just a little stressed out. It's not your fault. Your father and I are just…" she trailed off and didn't bother to finish. It was pointless. He didn't need to hear about it. That was the one thing she hated the most about their breakup. She could live without Richard in her life but it bothered the hell out of her that Jordan was playing piggy in the middle to their issues. She hadn't stopped to wonder how he was coping with it all. It couldn't have been easy.

* * *

Several hours later, and further south in Yellowstone, Logan made a trip to Lake Clinic to visit Hayden. The urgent care clinic was one of three in the park, the other two were in Mammoth and over at Old Faithful. In the event that patients needed to be transported out of the park, a helicopter would usually take them to Eastern Idaho Regional Medical Center, or one in Bozeman or Jackson Hole. Lake Clinic was located by the water, just west of the hotel dining room and post office. Logan stopped by the general store on the way in to pick up some coffee because the clinic's vending machine coffee tasted like mud. As the clinic only offered basic medical care, including stabilization of major trauma, he fully expected Hayden to be gone, but fortunately he was still there.

Logan rapped on his door. Hayden was upright in bed watching the news when he entered. "Hey buddy," Logan said. "How you doing?"

Hayden turned down the news.

He offered back a broad smile and his eyes lit up. All a good sign. "Ah, you brought me coffee. You're a lifesaver. I thought I was liable to die from the crap they serve up here," he said with a nod to the full cup of vending machine coffee on the side table.

"Well it was either that or I brought you flowers and I just couldn't seem to find those daisies that you like so much." He grinned and Hayden chuckled.

Logan glanced at the news. Media had arrived at the park after someone had leaked out a video of the dead fish in the lake.

"Damn strange, huh."

"You're telling me," Logan said. "We had a meeting last night with Harris and Hank. Did you know NASA was drilling in the park?"

Hayden nearly spat out his coffee. "Where?"

"Northeast, south, and west apparently. Harris was very tight-lipped about it. Seems they got the go-ahead last month. I've yet to see them but Harris says they're here."

"Isn't that the way? Only those at the top know what's going on and us minions at the bottom are the last to hear about it."

"That's what worries me," Logan said taking a seat and pulling his chair close to the bed. "Hank said his COSPEC readings were high over in Death Gulch. The same place he found those dead grizzlies."

Hayden blew on the surface of his drink and took a sip. "Are you serious?"

"I don't know what to believe. He called me this

morning to say he's heading out there with Catherine Shaw. He wants me to tag along."

"Catherine?"

Logan turned his attention away from the news. "Oh, some chick from the University of Utah. We all went out last night for drinks."

"Oh yeah," Hayden said getting a smirk on his face. "And how did it go after the drinks?"

Logan chuckled. "It wasn't like that."

"No? So what's she like?"

"You'll see." He looked at his watch. "She's meant to be showing up here in the next hour. I'm taking her up there along with a team from the USGS."

Hayden's face quickly went from a smirk to serious. "What's happening, Logan?"

"I'd like to say I know but I'm still confused. I'm leaning on their data, and depending on who you talk to, you get a different answer. USGS is confident that it's nothing more than the natural rumblings of the caldera. Shaw and Hank think otherwise."

"And you?"

He looked down into his coffee as steam rose to his face. "I think the park's trying to avoid crying wolf, and avoid political and economic problems. I don't like it, that's for sure. But not a lot I can do about it right now."

"Speaking of doing something about it. What's the update on that asshole? You caught him yet?"

"No. We have rangers in the park along with ISB looking for them. Handing out flyers to the public."

"Flyers?" Hayden laughed. "So they don't think twice about alerting the public to presence of a dangerous individual who could be long gone by now but they won't say a word about the sleeping giant beneath our feet."

"Crazy, right?" Logan said before taking another swig of his coffee and turning his attention back to the news. The news anchor was interviewing tourists about what they saw. A photo of the woman who lost her life on the lake came up on the screen. She left behind a husband and four kids.

"Damn shame. Strangest shit I've ever seen. You

know, I'm thinking of transferring out," Hayden said.

"To a different hospital?"

"No, you moron. Out of this job."

"C'mon, you love Yellowstone."

Hayden pulled a painful face as he adjusted himself. "No, I'm serious. I got talking with Allison. The wedding is next year and well with a baby on the way, I'm thinking maybe it's time I hang up the hat and find something a little less dangerous."

"You've got to be kidding me."

He shook his head. "Even Indiana Jones knew when to hang up his hat."

Logan laughed. "But I thought you lived for this shit."

"Yeah, until you find yourself bleeding out in the woods," he said looking down at his bandaged leg. "It gets you thinking about the bigger picture. You know I could have died out there, Logan." He looked down into his drink and closed his eyes.

"You sure Allison hasn't been putting pressure on you? Jenna did the same with me."

"No. Allison is quite the opposite. That girl gets off on hearing about all the dangerous situations I find myself in."

"Isn't that just the way?"

Hayden sighed as he looked back up at the TV. "Besides, this place is unstable. I mean, what other job puts you on top of a ticking time bomb and expects you to show up with a smile on your face and be grateful for seventeen bucks an hour? I got talking to my brother down in Florida. He wants me to come and work for him at his auto body shop. He said he would train me."

"Really?"

"Yeah. You remember you saying how we have to keep our eyes open for when opportunity knocks? Well I think that's opportunity knocking. I don't see myself doing this for much longer."

It was a real change of heart. Hayden had always been gung-ho to get out there and deal with the criminal element of Yellowstone. In fact he was originally keen to switch over and become a law enforcement ranger but when the opening came he never took it. He never thought he would see the day his friend would want to throw in the towel. It got Logan thinking about his own career. He loved doing what he did. There was a lot of freedom in it but at the same time there was more danger. Even more so than being a regular cop in the city. Here they didn't have the backup. They worked in remote areas where help could be an hour away. Besides troublemakers visiting the park they had to deal with the threat from wildlife like bears and cougars. They were twelve times more likely to be assaulted than a U.S. Border Patrol officer and twelve times more likely to be attacked than an FBI agent. Then of course there was the elephant in the room — Yellowstone itself. It didn't matter what the powers that be said about the likelihood of it not erupting. They didn't know for sure. Even though they had stations in and around Yellowstone tracking the sleeping beast, and global positioning systems to monitor ground deformation, they didn't know for sure if or when it would explode. That's why there was no evacuation plan in place. If they thought they had time, if they thought they had the luxury of a few weeks or months, they could draw up a plan to alert people on how to leave but he'd seen firsthand how they'd dealt with the forest fires. It was chaotic at best.

Logan nodded and patted his arm. "Well whatever you plan to do, I'm sure you'll land on your feet. That's just who you are."

"I appreciate that, man."

"And hey... I'm sorry if over the last few months if I've been a bit distant."

"You don't have to apologize to me. I get it, brother. This life is one wild ride and sometimes all you can do is hold on for dear life and hope your ass is still in the seat at the end."

They both laughed.

Right then there was a knock at the door. "Come in."

The door creaked open and Catherine stepped in. Hayden, in his usual man whore fashion, pulled himself up and ran a hand through his messy hair. "Wow, these nurses are getting better looking by the day."

"Hayden, this is Catherine Shaw."

"Ah, I've heard a lot about you."

"Good things, I hope?" she said extending her hand and diverting her gaze to Logan. He smiled and cleared his throat as he caught the aroma of her perfume. It had been a long while since he'd smelled someone so good. The park tended to attract folks that smelled like campfire smoke and the back end of a bison.

Chapter 13

Death Gulch was a gloomy ravine in the northeast corner of Yellowstone. It wasn't the first time animals had dropped dead in the area, hence the reason why Harris didn't immediately see the urgency of alerting visitors to the potential dangers of toxic gases venting from the volcano. Generally considered an area of the park where tourists didn't go, it had one time been full of hot springs but over the years the water no longer flowed from the vents. Now all that remained was a rocky gully with a small clear stream of cold water at the bottom that mixed with sulfuric acid.

The only ways to reach the area were by following 212 east through Lamar Valley and then hiking south along the Lamar River, or taking horses, or going by helicopter. Hank had made arrangements to take the USGS team out there first thing and then to swing back to collect Catherine and Logan.

Catherine wasn't keen on rubbing shoulders with Rebecca but she wasn't going to let it stop her from investigating further. Her work with the USGS had been a passion of hers. Getting boots on the ground and examining samples and monitoring activity was what she missed the most. She could have stayed on. No one forced her out of her position but with the short-lived affair that Richard had with Rebecca, the office drama over her involvement with the Long Valley Caldera, and her marriage falling apart, it had all taken its toll. It was just easier to be away but that meant being relegated to an office, staring at a screen, sitting in meetings and reviewing and editing scientific papers and reports. Preparing equipment and field deployment was handled by the USGS. Back when she was working for the USGS, a quarter of her time was spent in the field making observations, collecting specialized data and conducting surveys. Though that was mostly in the summer, the winter months made it hard due to snow.

On the way out Hank rode shotgun in the front of the

Bell 206 Jet Ranger helicopter. It seated up to four people. Catherine and Logan were in the back.

"Where's Jordan today?" Logan asked over the steady thump of the rotor blades.

She raised her voice so he could hear her. "I pulled a few strings to have him join one of the ranger program tours for a couple of hours."

"And he agreed?"

She frowned. "Strangely enough, yeah. As long as the tour is not with his mother, he seems as happy as a clam."

Logan nodded thoughtfully. "Sorry to hear that."

"Ah, don't worry. I'm used to it." She glanced out the window.

"So he doesn't live with you?"

"No, I'm based in Utah, and he and his father are out in California. His schooling is out there and after we separated it just seemed like a lot to ask him to give up his friends and everything that is familiar to him. Then of course there was the fact that Richard is a cop and he had a lot more sway with the courts. Contrary to what most think, it's not always the wife that ends up with the kids. Though looking back on it now I think the worst mistake I made was moving out before we got divorced. It made me look like I was abandoning the family. I didn't know the courts frowned upon that. Crazy, right?"

He nodded. "Things don't always go to plan."

"And you?"

"I was set to marry Jenna. She had these big plans to have a family, settle out east and live in a small town close to her parents." He breathed in deeply.

"Did you know her long?"

"Four years. She was camping when I met her."

"You think you would have liked to have kids?"

"You don't miss what you've never had, right?"

Catherine squinted. "I guess."

They both looked out as they flew over the hilly landscape of rock and fir trees. It was beautiful to see it from above and it only served to remind her of how large Yellowstone was. They were seeing just a tiny fraction. The thought of it all being wiped out in one fell swoop was overwhelming. The odds of an eruption were low but then it was for Mount St. Helens, too. She thought back to the photo that was taken just minutes before it erupted. For all their experience and technology, Mother Nature demonstrated her unpredictability.

"If it did blow, what kind of devastation are we looking at?" Logan asked. "I mean, I understand 87,000 would be wiped out instantly but is that it?"

"It depends."

"On what?"

"Are we talking about a full eruption or just a small one that pushes lava out like toothpaste?"

"A full," Logan said.

"It's speculative at best right now but a column of ash and lava would shoot upwards to around sixteen miles high with the molten layer traveling as far as 500 to 1,000 miles away. Hot scalding ash would be pumped into the jet streams and be transported around the stratosphere. It would move at speeds of up to 300 miles an hour. A mixture of ash, lava blebs and superheated gas at temperatures higher than 1,832 celsius would kill people within seconds and burn those beyond as the air heats up. Anyone within the national park, and surrounding states would no doubt be wiped out. Though that's just from the initial blast. The ash fallout would be colossal. You are looking at something that is six times denser than water so buildings would collapse under its weight, roads and sewer systems would clog up and break down. Water supplies would be contaminated, and the electrical grid would short out. Air travel would be suspended. Sending out search and rescue teams would be pointless, as the area would be blanketed in high levels of volcanic residue. Two thirds of the United States would be uninhabitable." She took a breath and glanced out then squinted from the glare of the sun. "Even the smallest amount of ash would travel as far as Calgary, Winnipeg, Chicago, Toronto, Washington, D.C., and New York, and essentially send the United States into a volcanic winter. FEMA would be cleaning up for months, even years after. The death toll is hard to predict but it's clear the devastation would be vast." She took a deep breath. "But that wouldn't be the worst of it. All that ash injected into the stratosphere would cause the skies to darken and the temperature to cool. That could affect the world as a whole, if only by a few degrees Celsius. You see when Pinatubo erupted back in 1991, it cooled down the planet by about 1 degree Celsius for a few years. And when Tambora in Indonesia back in 1815 occurred, it was so devastating it disrupted the weather system and cooled the planet enough to damage crops, and cause epidemic disease and civil unrest around the world. That's why 1816 was known as 'The Year Without Summer'. And those were fairly small eruptions in comparison to what could happen with Yellowstone." Catherine glanced out the window as they got closer to Death Gulch. "It wouldn't just be life, weather and agriculture that would be affected. It would damage the economy. An eruption could put the total U.S. damage at around three trillion dollars. So, while it may not be the end of life on the planet it could certainly throw the United States back into the dark ages and into a volcanic winter. Now having said that, that's going on the basis that we experienced a full eruption, a complete unzipping of the caldera."

Logan grimaced. "So with all things said, the future would be bright."

Catherine chuckled and shook her head.

The pilot brought the helicopter down into a flat area where many of the trees had died. It was a very eerie feeling as they touched ground and looked out at the barren wasteland. It was a stark comparison to the lush, rich greenery found elsewhere in the park.

"Here, put this on," Hank said twisting around and handing them each a gas mask.

"Are you serious?" Logan asked.

"It's your lungs."

He took it and all three of them ducked out from beneath the whip of the rotors and made their way over to a group of three team members from the USGS who were waiting nearby.

"Where's Rebecca?" Catherine asked noticing she

wasn't with them.

"She's with the van back at Highway 212," Mark Bowman replied.

"Oh, poor woman. Did she not want to break a heel?" Catherine said in jest. Mark gave a nod of his head towards an area where they'd set up their instruments. They were planning on doing some tests and then heading to the northeast side of the park to see what NASA was doing.

"Hank, were the bears the only animals you saw?" Mark asked.

"Yeah, why?"

"Looks like we have some more."

He led them down into the gulch. It was a steep incline, rocky and treacherous. Most of it was white, decomposed rock with small oozes of water coming from the slopes. Steam spiraled up from areas, and a thick, creamy, white deposit covered what was left of the stream bed below. As they came around a large field of boulders, they noticed further down inside the gulch the carcasses of some more bears, along with elk, and small animals like squirrels and hares. "Oh, God, that's awful," Hank said.

"We've also been getting an increase in micro earthquakes. Multiple over the last hour." Mark led them over to an open laptop that was hooked up to a seismic monitor.

"Have you been down to check on the carcasses?" Hank asked.

"What, to see if they're fresh? They look fresh to me."

"No, to take samples."

"No, we've had our hands full."

With that said he got on the radio to the van, and Catherine heard Rebecca's annoying voice. It was just like her to send her team in while she hung back, probably sipping on a latte and scrolling through her social media feed. The woman was a total diva. Catherine had some ideas of how she'd managed to wiggle her way into the position as scientist-in-charge. She thought about those in office who would sit slack-jawed as she wore a low-cut dress and gave presentations at the front of a boardroom.

The lack of concentration was a surefire giveaway.

"Well I'm heading down," Hank said.

"I'll go with you," Catherine said, eager to take a closer look. Logan followed as they pitched sideways and worked their way around boulders and what remained of trees. The site looked as if a plane had swooped down and cut into the earth, tearing up the soil, and snapping trees in half.

"Hank, have you been over to see the equipment NASA is using?"

"Yeah. Though they didn't let me get very close."

"And so you've seen a correlation between the seismic activity and the time of when they started drilling?" Catherine asked.

"Yeah."

"And you didn't say anything?" Logan asked looking almost dumbfounded.

"Of course I did but my words fell on deaf ears. You know how things operate around here better than anyone else, Logan."

As they got closer to the carcasses, the smell of death lingered in the air. Hank said there was a possibility that animals were dropping dead in this location because of the concentration of gas emanations, and the way the gulch trapped it in. Hank crouched down, slipped on a pair of blue latex gloves and examined the bear. "No signs of bullet wounds, or any marks of injury, and there is no sense that it died from violence but there are a few drops of dried blood beneath its nose."

"Same over here," Catherine said.

"And here," Logan muttered.

While a few of the carcasses were decayed, the rest were fresh, indicating they hadn't died that long ago.

"It's possible the bear made its way down after catching the scent of the dead animals and was asphyxiated by the gas trapped in the pocket of the gulch." Catherine removed her mask for a second to get a sense of what they were dealing with. A strong smell of sulfur overwhelmed her, almost instantly choking her even though a strong wind blew through the gulch. She covered her face, and then took samples.

Logan rose and cast a glance around shaking his head. "I'm going to head up and speak with Mark," Logan said. "I want to know what ideas they have about the fish in the lake, and to check if anyone has been there yet." Catherine gave a nod and continued to gather a few earth samples; she wanted to compare them with different samples taken throughout the park.

"Hank," Catherine said.

"Yeah?"

"If we are on the brink of an eruption we won't have a lot of time to evacuate people. If you are even the slightest bit unsure about the stability of the caldera, I would suggest having the superintendent put this park on evacuation notification."

"I'm afraid I'm not the one with the final word. What I say carries weight but ultimately it comes down to the USGS."

She sighed. That meant relying on Rebecca to make the call and she had a habit of holding back to avoid marring her name. It was less about how the businesses in the surrounding area would suffer if it was a false alert, and more about maintaining her flawless status as scientist-in-charge. She sighed. Worst-case scenario, at least if Hank saw that trouble was brewing, together they might be able to convince the superintendent to at least reconsider.

She screwed the top on a steel sample container closed and pocketed it. "Well, once we compare these with a few areas on the northeast, west and south, we should have a better idea of what is going on. Let's head up," she said.

"Be right with you."

Catherine began working her way up the precarious V-shaped trench that was just less than seventy-five feet deep. She hadn't made it ten yards when a noticeable rumble began. At first the shaking was very subtle, then it got stronger, and stronger. Boulders gave way and came rolling down causing her to leap out of the way. Further down, Hank was trying to steady himself against one of the dead bears. Catherine figured it would stop soon but it didn't. It continued and grew in strength until the whole gulch was shaking violently. What came next was shocking. Like steel beams snapping on a bridge, a fissure formed in the center of the gulch stretching down, opening like a pair of lips to reveal its rocky teeth.

"Hank!" she yelled.

He tried to move but the ground was shaking too hard and he lost his balance, landing on top of the lifeless bear. In the next second, the bear dropped into the rocky abyss. The last thing Catherine heard was Hank cry out. Grit shot into the air along with a plume of dust making it hard to see anything. Catherine hung on to a large boulder for dear life. She could hear Logan calling out to her but couldn't make out what he was saying. In that moment fear took over. *This is it. This is it,* she told herself. The caldera was about to explode and in a matter of seconds she would be gone.

But it wasn't it.

Molten lava didn't emerge from the 200-foot fissure, and when they didn't think the shaking would stop, it did, like a light switch being turned off. Still clinging to the boulder, Catherine looked down through the murky deluge of steam, dust and grit for Hank. All she could see was the giant gaping crack in the earth.

"Catherine, wait!" Logan yelled from further up. But she didn't wait. She scrambled down, nearly losing her footing and tumbling forward. She somehow managed to avoid going head first into the ground. Without brushing off the grime, she got back up and continued on down calling out to Hank but getting no reply. When she made it to the edge of the fissure she waved a hand in front of her face to clear the air of dust.

"Hank!"

She moved further up the crack searching for him. All the while Logan and the team were making their way down. She could hear them calling out to her to be careful but she wasn't thinking of her own safety in that moment. She just wanted to find him.

Seconds passed, then minutes before she spotted him buried beneath dead animals and rocks. She could tell that if he wasn't dead, he was badly injured as the rocks and weight of the animals had pinned him in and blood was trickling down into the steaming crack. "Hank! Hank!"

Logan caught up with her and pulled her back.

"No. Get off."

"Catherine. Let me go and check."

She took a few steps back while Mark tossed a yellow rope to Logan and they tied it around two trees before he threw the rest into the crack and he went over to check Hank's vitals. Maria, one of the other USGS team members, wrapped an arm around her.

It was a tense few minutes as Logan worked his way down to Hank.

Then what she feared the most came true.

"Pull me up. He's gone."

Chapter 14

Rangers were everywhere but that was to be expected even on a normal day. Yellowstone had over 773 rangers in the peak of summer, most were permanent, and the rest were brought in from other parks to carry the weight of the heaviest tourist season. Even though Billy was familiar with how they operated because he'd grown up spending most of his teen years in the area of Yellowstone, and had an uncle who worked for them at one time, seeing this many on the road was unnerving. They were usually spread out throughout the park doing mundane jobs like giving tours, maintaining trails, cleaning up graffiti, protecting the park and people, dealing with wildlife, interpreting, manning the entrance points, providing directions, and generally giving out the same useless information to clueless tourists. There was no way in hell he would have done the job. He saw the kind of crap they had to take from groups of drunks, and the risks they took when they came under fire by a trigger-happy protester. But as long as there were national parks there would always be those in khaki pants and funny hats.

They were crouched down in the tree line not far from Bridge Bay Marina watching an unusual scene play out. The parking lot was packed with vehicles. Every parking space was taken up, many filled with news vans with antennas on the top. Cables snaked out of vans across the lot over to the dock where hundreds of curious onlookers watched as if preparing for a big fireworks display.

"What's the media doing here?" Wyatt asked.

"Better question, how the hell did they manage to catch that many fish?"

Several large boats hauled in nets of fish, emptying them out along the wooden docks. There had to be thousands inside the netting. In all his years visiting the park Billy had never seen anyone bring in that many. There had been some impressive catches when they ran tournaments but those paled in comparison to the pile of fish before them.

"Well, who cares? It makes for the perfect distraction. One of these vehicles has to have a gasoline canister. We might even find a full one."

"Yeah, and maybe we'll escape the strong arm of the law," Wyatt said sarcastically, then dashed out of the tree line at a crouch. The parking lot was about a hundred yards from the forested area. They'd agreed that Wyatt would go in just in case Billy was spotted. He didn't think they'd be able to identify him as he'd already changed out of his clothes into ones stolen from Bridge Bay Campsite, but he wasn't taking any chances. He chuckled to himself at the thought of some unlucky soul returning to his tent to find a pair of jeans, a sweater, a jacket, forty bucks, and a packet of smokes gone. Billy tapped out one, and lit it. He inhaled deeply letting the nicotine calm his anxiety. His eyes darted between the rangers dealing with crowd control and Wyatt who was checking the back of trucks for a gasoline can.

Several minutes passed and Wyatt disappeared out of view.

Billy nervously tapped his fingers against his knee and bit down on his lower lip. "C'mon. C'mon," he mumbled. He shifted position trying to get a bead on where Wyatt had gone. The parking lot was huge and because there were so many vehicles he figured he was farther down. As he moved along the tree line he noticed a female ranger peering over the heads of a group of young teens. She seemed to be focused on the parking lot.

"Shit." Billy watched as she squeezed her way through the crowd heading for the lot. Had she seen Wyatt? If so, why hadn't she called for assistance from some of the other rangers nearby? *Think. Think.* He thought of calling out to him but that would have only given away his position. The ranger pressed on, slipping through the masses. No. They couldn't afford to get caught. Not now. Not after Wyatt came back. Against his better judgment, Billy dashed out and sprinted across the open field into the parking lot, his eyes scanning for his friend. He was nowhere to be found. "Wyatt?" he said in a hushed tone. No response. He slipped passed multiple vehicles, looking both ways. It was like being in a huge open store, glancing down aisles.

Billy ducked behind a truck as the ranger came into view heading to the north end of the lot. *Damn it.* He rounded the end of the truck and broke into a sprint while staying low. Wyatt had to be at the far end. No sooner had he made it six vehicles down than he spotted him in the back of a truck rooting around.

Without even saying his name, he hopped up onto the truck and pounced on him bringing him down hard. The truck's suspension bounced a little. With his hand clamped over his mouth he whispered into his ear to stay quiet and slip out the end of the truck. Quickly they hopped out and ran at a crouch. They had just ducked behind a vehicle when they heard the ranger's voice.

"I see you there. Come on out."

Billy squeezed his eyes tight. The last thing he wanted was to have to hurt another ranger — especially a woman. He slowly reached down for his knife, taking a firm grip on the handle.

"You're not fooling anyone. Now unless you want to get into further trouble then I recommend you step out."

Wyatt glanced at Billy and he shook his head. His mind was churning over their options. He could round the front of the truck while Wyatt distracted her and then creep up behind her. She wouldn't know what hit her, or…

"Jordan, get out here now!"

Both of them frowned. *Jordan?*

Billy lowered himself to the gravel surface and looked beneath the truck. One truck over he saw the suspension bounce a little and then a pair of white Nikes hit the ground.

"Your mother is going to hear about this."

"Whatever," the kid said as the ranger clasped hold of him and led him away.

Billy breathed a sigh of relief, and then he started chuckling. "For a minute there I thought our number was up. I was just about to go all Michael Myers on her ass."

Wyatt let out a deep belly laugh and slapped him on

the back. "We've been in this park far too long."

"You're telling me. Did you find a gasoline canister?"

"Actually I found something even better."

Wyatt reached into his pocket and pulled out a set of keys and dangled them in front of his face.

"What are those for?"

"A black 4 x 4 Ford truck, the one I was in before you rudely dragged me out."

"Hey, I was saving your ass." He frowned, looking confused. "Where were they?"

"Inside the truck. The owner must have shut it off and forgot to collect them. So it looks like we won't be needing that gasoline."

"Of course we will, you idiot. We can't drive out of here in a stolen truck. You know how fast they would catch us? The owner is probably on his way back to find them. Go take them back."

"No, we can drive out of here. They won't be expecting us to drive out the east gate."

Billy groaned and slapped his forehead. "They're

looking for two guys. Now if word gets out that a black Ford truck is missing, and they still have those roadblocks in place, what do you think will happen?" He paused for a second and when he didn't get a response he continued. "Exactly, so let's put the keys back and just siphon the gasoline out."

"Using what, our mouths?"

Billy rolled his eyes as he got up and reached over into the truck they were hiding behind, withdrew an empty five-gallon canister, and dropped it in his lap. "There we go."

"Oh c'mon, I checked nine different vehicles and the first one you look in has it?"

"What can I say? I have the luck of the Irish."

"But you're not Irish."

"Then things must be really looking up." He smiled and they made their way back to the truck. Billy kept watch as he put the keys back into the 4 x 4. Once it was done they strolled along the back of the vehicles, heading for the tree line. They were five yards from the end of the parking lot when Billy dragged Wyatt to the ground.

"What?"

He didn't say anything but looked toward where he left the dirt bike. There were two park rangers examining it, along with his backpack, which he'd left behind. They had pulled out his wingsuit. One of them got on the radio while the other one looked around. All they could do was watch as the ranger hauled the bike up and led it away.

"Oh, you have got to be joking!" Billy placed his head in his hand.

"Well that settles that," Wyatt said. "I guess we're taking the truck."

* * *

The journey over to US-212 was a solemn one. Logan couldn't bring Hank up as he was pinned beneath two large boulders and it would require equipment they didn't have. He radioed through to search and rescue and the team reassured him they would head out there as soon as possible. They were currently dealing with two lost hikers on the east side.

The pilot brought the helicopter down near a rest area along the northeast entrance road. It was a barren spot in the park just north of Death Gulch and the location that Rebecca and one of the other members of the USGS team had chosen. They were working out of a white van packed with seismic instruments and high-end computer equipment.

Catherine glanced out the window and saw Rebecca standing beside the van in cream-colored khaki pants, and a tight V-neck T-shirt that was bursting at the seams. Her hands were clasped behind her back, her chin out as if readying for an onslaught of questions. Beside her was Kyle Davenport, her lap dog.

They felt the helicopter jolt a little before it finally settled on the ground. Logan and Catherine slipped out and stayed low as the wind whipped their clothes. Within seconds the helicopter took off again to collect the other three USGS team members.

"I heard what happened. I'm sorry," were the first words out of her mouth. As much as Catherine appreciated her humanity, it hadn't made her forget the danger of the situation.

"You need to speak to the superintendent. There is far too much activity happening. The seismic readings were off the charts."

"We're getting nothing right now," Rebecca said leading them into the back of the van to show them what they had found.

Kyle tore off a sheet of data and handed it to Catherine. On it, she could see the same readings printed out back in Death Gulch except now it had returned to normal. She handed it back. "I'm telling you, Rebecca. This caldera is awakening and…"

"And… we are here to monitor, collect data and then decide what course of action to take. I will not have a repeat of Mammoth Lakes."

"You mean you won't risk your career?"

Rebecca narrowed her gaze and then told Kyle to hop into the driver's seat and get ready to take them back to the main headquarters in the north end of the park as soon as the others returned.

"That's it?" Catherine said.

"Did I say that was it?" she replied staring back at her. "Look, I know you were close to Hank. We all—"

"Please. Don't say you were."

She opened her mouth to speak then closed it. A couple of seconds passed before she continued, "I'm just saying that until we have taken readings from the seismograph stations, observed the thermal activity and spoken with NASA we cannot form a definitive decision."

"Hank was sure."

"Well I'm not," she snapped.

"Thousands of lives are on the line, Rebecca."

"And so is the economy and livelihood of communities in and around Yellowstone." She paused. "I will not have you pushing your own agenda."

"My agenda? And what would that be?"

"Trying to prove I was wrong all along."

Catherine snorted. "Believe it or not, Rebecca, not everything is about you."

She hopped out of the van to get some air. Rebecca hollered, "You do your job and we'll do ours."

Before heading back to the headquarters in Mammoth they were planning on visiting the northeast quarter of the park. NASA had positioned one of its drilling rigs not far from the entrance in a mountainous landscape called Republic Mountain just south of Silver Gate. They couldn't leave until the others returned, all of which meant biting her tongue. Between Rebecca, Richard, the activity and Yellowstone, it was making for one hell of a getaway. She took a seat on the curb a good distance away from the van to think about Hank. He'd always been nice to her, treated her with respect and on the same level. There were few geologists that were like that, and now they were short one more.

Logan stepped out of the van and muttered something to them before scanning the lot. He strolled over with his hands in his pockets, gazing around him. "You okay?" he asked, putting one foot up on the curb and placing an elbow on his knee.

Catherine wiped away a tear. "I will be once she's out of my face."

He snorted. "There is always one bad apple among the bunch."

"Isn't that the truth? I've never been sure what her deal is."

"It's called ego."

Catherine smiled.

"I can't believe he's gone." Logan said. "I'm gonna miss that old coot."

She was about to reply when her phone began vibrating in her pocket. She fished it out and answered.

"Yes?"

It was the ranger in charge of the tour her son was on. "Ms. Shaw, I don't want you to get worried but… Jordan has gone missing."

Chapter 15

Their nerves were on edge as they drove east out of Bridge Bay Marina's parking lot, sticking to Highway 14. A strong wind blew against the vehicle causing a whistling noise because one of the windows was partly open. Wyatt drove while Billy stayed low on the passenger side covered with a blanket.

"Are you sure you don't want to go north? It would save a lot of time."

"No, we head for Cody."

On a good day with average traffic it would take roughly two hours. By that point they would be outside of the national park and no one would be searching for them. Billy looked up at Wyatt who kept adjusting his hands on the wheel. His knuckles had turned white.

"You've jumped out of an airplane, bungee jumped and wingsuit dived at low elevations and yet you look like you're going to shit yourself."

Wyatt didn't break a smile. He shot him a glance and swallowed hard. "What do we do if we come across a checkpoint?"

"Play it cool. They aren't going to search vehicles."

"Yes they are. They were doing it in the west."

"Right," Billy said, clenching his teeth. In all fairness he hadn't really given thought to what they would say if they were stopped. He touched the handle of the knife in the sheath on the side of his waist — that knife was the only plan he had and he didn't want to use it.

"They can't have every road blocked," Billy said.

"We are on a main through road so unless you have a plan, we might have to go off road."

"So we go off road but we'll deal with that when we come to it."

Wyatt nodded and looked down at him. Every so often he would glance at him. Billy knew he wanted to say something but he didn't.

"What is it?" Billy asked.

"Nothing."

"You're not very good at lying."

He breathed in deeply. "What if the ranger you stabbed is dead?"

Billy studied his friend's face. He could see fear and concern had got the better of him. It wasn't that Billy didn't care about the consequences of his actions, it was just he'd spent so many years dodging authority figures, he'd formed a belief that he was untouchable. But was that what Wyatt was worried about?"

"It was just a flesh wound."

"Really?"

"Yeah." Billy nodded, trying to convince him that it wasn't a big deal. Wyatt changed his mind all the time and the last thing he needed was for him to fall back into panic. That had been the reason why he'd driven away the night before. The truth was the ranger might be dead. He'd driven that knife deep into his thigh. He saw the blood gushing out and soaking his pants as he fled. In that moment he didn't think about if he would live or die, he just wanted to escape and get far away from trouble.

"Anyway, where are we now?"

"Just coming around Indian Pond. The road is clear so far. We might actually be in luck."

"Yeah like I said. You worry about a whole bunch of nothing."

No sooner had the words spilled out of his mouth than Wyatt eased off the gas, slowing the vehicle and bringing it onto the hard shoulder.

"What is it?"

"A roadblock."

"You're kidding."

"Billy, do I look like it?" he said gripping the steering wheel tighter. "We'll have to go back."

"We can't go back to Bridge Bay."

"No, there was a trail back there near the pond." With that said he did a U-turn and drove for another few minutes before he left the road again. Billy rose and looked out the window. They were barreling down a dirt trail that went parallel to Highway 14, then it took a sharp turn north.

"Do you know where you're going?" Billy asked.

"No but we are out of options."

The terrain was full of wide-open spaces of greenery, then patches of dense woodland. They drove for what felt like thirty minutes and didn't see a single vehicle or ranger. Billy pulled out his phone and tried to get a signal but there was nothing. The further north they went the thicker the woods became. The trail appeared to have been formed over time through constant use but then some parts were thick with undergrowth indicating that no one had been out this way in a while.

"How we doing for gas?"

"That's the one thing going for us," Wyatt said. He tapped the fuel gauge. "Unless this isn't working."

"Don't jinx it," Billy said pulling out a cigarette and lighting it. He offered Wyatt one and he took it. "Well you know what, Wyatt. This will make one hell of a story to tell your grandkids one day."

They both laughed.

"Anyway, how's Rita doing?"

"You mean, is she still mad at you?" Wyatt replied, his lip curling up.

"That as well."

"She hasn't mentioned your name in a while but that doesn't mean you are in the clear."

Wyatt had been dating Rita since their school years. He already had two kids and she was pregnant with their third. At one time she was pretty cool about them going out and doing crazy things like sky diving and jumping off cliffs, but with their third on the way she'd begun applying the brakes on their ventures and nagging Wyatt to get a real job. That's why he let Wyatt go after stabbing the ranger. He didn't want him getting into trouble and they had come close to it over the past few years.

"You know she won't ever let you come out again with me after this."

"She isn't going to know about this!" Wyatt said, flashing his pearly whites. "If we get out of this, it's time to settle down, Billy. I'm heading out to Maine and starting afresh and I think you should do the same."

Billy wasn't dating anyone, though that didn't mean he slept alone. That was the upswing to their job and the reason he wasn't keen to do anything else. Although they didn't show their entire faces on video, people could hear their voices, and he didn't think twice about whipping out his phone when he was in a bar and showing the ladies. At first they would blow him off and say he was full of it and then he would pull out the bandanna worn in the video, tie it around his face and repeat something said in a video and he'd watch their eyes widen. Like goddamn, he felt like Zorro, the people's man, well that was if Zorro was real, an adrenaline junkie, and had a massive online following.

He was lost in the memories of days gone by and enjoying his cigarette when Wyatt leaned over and tapped him on the arm. "Hey, look." He pointed up ahead to a rugged log cabin that was nestled into a large diamond-shaped patch of woods. For the most part the terrain on either side of them was wide and nothing more than dusty landscape. "This is a little off the beaten path to have a campsite."

"That's not a campsite. It's an old ranger cabin. Most national parks have them. They built them back in the 1920s and '30s. Not all of them are in use anymore but some are." There was no vehicle outside.

"You want to stop?"

"No, keep going."

The road curved as it got closer to the cabin and continued north, cutting up through a mountainous region called Pelican Cone. They drove on for another twenty minutes until they found themselves on a steep incline heading down into what seemed like a canyon. Wyatt yapped on about Maine, and buying a house by the water, and recounted all the tales his uncle had told him about how great life was out there. He made it sound like the gold rush era except the gold was fish and it was easier to find. As they came over a rise in the trail, Wyatt slammed the brakes causing Billy to jerk forward and nearly go head first through the windshield. About to go nuclear on his ass, he looked out to see what the problem was and saw the road was blocked. Though this time it wasn't a checkpoint — large boulders had cascaded into the canyon floor cutting out any viable way of continuing on.

"Shit! I swear someone up there has it in for me," Billy said balling his hand and banging the dashboard. He opened the door and got out and kicked the side of the truck a few times before walking over and climbing up on the boulders. Wyatt joined him and looked at the steam rising through the cracks. In some spots there was smoke.

"That doesn't look good."

Billy looked up the rocky slopes. "Must have been another earthquake."

"More reason to get the hell out of here," Wyatt said turning and heading back to the truck. They didn't waste time. Wyatt reversed and turned the vehicle around and gave it some gas heading back the way they came. He was sure he saw a turnoff a few miles back. Billy began fishing around inside the glove compartment.

"What are you searching for?"

"Water. I'm thirsty."

"I think there is some back there behind your seat."

Billy twisted around and looked but there was nothing. He groaned.

"Look, let's stop at this cabin. It might be stocked."

"And it might have a ranger. And knowing our luck it will."

Wyatt laughed. "Such a pessimist. All the rangers are out looking for us. No one is coming out here." He veered off the road causing a plume of dust to swirl behind them and crossed over a small driveway that led up to the rustic cabin. They parked outside a few feet from the porch and Wyatt hopped out.

"Well you coming?"

Billy nodded and grabbed up his rifle. He wasn't taking any chances. The door was locked but a few hard kicks and it soon gave way, swinging wide. Inside there wasn't much to the place. A bed in a loft-style area accessible by a wooden ladder. A musty smelling couch, and a rocking chair. In the rear was another room with a table that had some kind of contraption on it covered by a sheet. There was a shelf with a few old books, and the kitchen had a sink and counter with a couple of cupboards. It was equipped with electric lights, electric stove, and a wood stove for heating up the place. But there was no drinking water. "Great," Billy said.

"There is a stream not far from here. And I'll go check the rear of the truck. I think I saw a cooler. Hopefully there's beer." He smiled as he headed out. Billy fished through the cupboards but they were empty. Not even a can of Spam. A cockroach scuttled across the ground nearby and he crushed it beneath his boot. He climbed up into the sleeping area and ducked some of the big spider webs. What a dive. It was clear no one had been there in years. He bonked his head on one of the rafters and cursed under his breath. This wasn't how he saw the trip playing out. It was meant to be seven days of eating good, eluding the rangers, filming some crazy stunts on their bikes and drinking beer.

Suddenly, Wyatt yelled.

Billy hurried over to a small dusty window and looked out. He ran his hand across the thick layer of dust to see Wyatt chasing someone. "What the hell?"

By the time he made it down and was out the door, Wyatt was halfway back clutching a young kid in both arms. One glance at his white Nike sneakers and he knew who it was.

"Get off me, man!" the kid yelled.

"Stop resisting."

He was wriggling around in his arms as Wyatt dropped him to the ground.

The scared kid looked up at them as they stared down.

"Found him in the back of the truck under a tarp."

"What the hell are you doing, kid?" Billy asked.

"I should ask you the same thing. I'm pretty sure that isn't your vehicle."

"How the hell would you know?"

"Because I saw the family who got out of it."

Wyatt looked at Billy and then back at the kid.

"Get up. Head into the cabin."

"I'm not going with you. You could be perverts."

Billy laughed then pointed his gun at him. "You're right, we could be. You're still going inside, Jordan."

"How do you know my name?"

"Ah, we know a lot, kid."

He'd remembered the ranger calling out his name when she was looking for him. Billy figured he must have given the gal the slip again and doubled back to the parking lot. Jordan got up and brushed off grime, gave them a dirty look then trudged on into the cabin.

Wyatt continued to fish through the belongings in the back while Billy had a heart to heart with the kid. "So what were you doing in the back?"

"Jerking off. What do you think?"

Billy's lip curled up. "Do you know the owner of the vehicle?"

"Somewhat. Let me tell you he's going to be super pissed off to find it gone."

"I bet he will. So why didn't you jump out?"

"Decided to snag a ride out of this shithole," Jordan said, walking around the inside and taking a seat in the rocking chair. He rocked back and forth looking at Billy through narrowed eyes.

"Ah, a disgruntled visitor. How old are you, kid?"

"13, going on 14."

"You seem a little young to be doing solo traveling. Where's your family?"

"California."

Billy leaned against the frame of the door, studying him. He lowered his rifle and pulled a cigarette out.

"You think I can get one of those?"

Billy laughed. "Your parents know you smoke?"

"They don't know much about me. Too busy fighting."

"Ah so that's how it is." Billy hesitated for a second but then thought, what the hell. He started when he was eleven. He'd steal cigarettes from his old man after a hard night at the bar. He tossed one over along with a box of matches. He watched the kid light it and take the first puff. It was easy to tell if someone hadn't smoked, they were usually coughing their lungs out on the first hit. Not this kid.

He tossed the matches back. "Thanks."

"You don't seem too worried."

Jordan shrugged.

"So how did you end up here?"

"How does anyone end up here? My mother who doesn't live with me decided it would be a great idea to go browsing on top of an active volcano."

He took a hard pull on his cigarette.

"Active? It's dormant, kid."

"Not anymore it isn't."

Chapter 16

"How the hell did this happen?" Catherine yelled over the phone. Logan looked at her as she walked a short distance away trying to make sense of the message.

"He was with the group and one of the families forgot the keys in their truck and he offered to go back and get them. After thirty minutes he didn't return so I went searching for him and found him on his phone in the back of another truck. I figured he had the keys and was just wasting time. When I returned him to the group he said he'd forgotten the keys and offered to go back again but the owner said he would head over there after he'd been to the washroom. I turned my back for a few seconds to deal with two unruly teens and he was gone. I headed back to the parking lot and the truck was gone. Dan, the owner, thinks he's taken it on a joyride."

Catherine couldn't comprehend this. This wasn't like him. Or was it? Had she been so focused on her new life away from Richard and Jordan that she had overlooked this? Was she to blame? She shook her head. "He wouldn't do that. He doesn't know how to drive."

"You'd be surprised how easy it is and in a place like this—"

"Terri, my son doesn't know how to drive and I think someone would have said something if they saw a thirteen-year-old tearing down the road."

"Look, I just called to let you know. We have rangers out looking right now and I've contacted search and rescue but it's going to take them time to get up here."

"I'm on my way."

"But…"

Before the ranger could finish, Catherine had hung up on her. She updated Logan on what was happening and he said he would go with her. Rebecca acted like she cared but Catherine knew differently. They had to wait another fifteen minutes before the helicopter arrived with the rest of the team and then instead of heading to see what operation NASA was running, they hopped in and headed south.

Rebecca's parting words were, "Don't you worry. Leave this in my hands."

Yeah, that's what worries me, she thought. The trip back to Bridge Bay seemed far longer than when they came. Catherine's mind churned over at the thought of her son getting lost in the backcountry. Visitors had been mauled by bears and then there were crazy people that often frequented national parks; the rapists, the drunks and… She turned to Logan who was looking out. "Logan, what's the update on the guy who stabbed Hayden?"

"No idea. As far as I'm aware they're still out there looking for them but resources are being stretched right now due to the lake issue and they can't put one hundred percent into that either because we still have to protect visitors and make sure nothing else happens."

"Well how does this work when someone goes missing in the park?"

"Search and rescue will do an aerial and ground search. Hopefully they can pinpoint the black truck. You can be sure the rangers will all be notified to be on the lookout. The upside, if you can think this way, is we usually don't have checkpoints throughout the park but because we're looking for this guy and his buddy, that's going to make it harder for someone driving that truck to drive out of the park."

Catherine nodded as she looked into her hands. Logan placed a hand on her shoulder. "We'll find him."

She nodded and managed to muster a faint smile.

* * *

Wyatt entered the cabin with a cooler in one hand, and a beer in the other. He tossed a beer to Billy, and he caught it before it hit the ground.

"Do I get one?" Jordan asked.

"Hell no, kid," Wyatt said before setting the cooler on the ground and kicking the door closed. "You hungry?" Wyatt asked reaching into the cooler and fishing out some sandwiches and several packets of chips. He tossed some onto Jordan's lap and gave one to Billy before he unwrapped his own.

"So what's your deal?" Wyatt asked him.

"He's running away. They didn't let him ride the pony," Billy said before cracking up laughing.

Jordan scowled at him.

"You don't like your old man?" Wyatt asked taking a large bite out of a cheese sandwich.

Jordan scowled. "No, we get along just fine. It's my mother."

"Yeah? What is she, a drug addict? Does she beat you?" Billy asked.

"No."

"So she shows your siblings more attention than you?"

He frowned. "No."

"Then what is it?"

He stared down at his sandwich then looked at them but dodged the question. "Why did you steal the vehicle?"

"Because the keys were inside."

"That's kind of dumb, isn't it?"

Billy smiled and looked at Wyatt. "I told you it was."

Wyatt shook his head and looked out a window. "We

didn't have any other options."

"Well how did you get in here?" Jordan asked, tapping his cigarette and acting all calm and collected.

"Why's he smoking?" Wyatt asked.

"Like you care?" Billy shot him a glance.

Wyatt shrugged.

"So?" Jordan asked, probing for details.

"We killed a ranger. That's right, kid. Stuck him like a pig in cold blood."

Jordan laughed nervously. "Are you serious?"

Wyatt looked at Billy knowing he was lying. Billy wanted to see what kind of reaction he could get out of him. "Yeah. And I'll kill anyone else who comes near us. Even kids." He burst out laughing and Wyatt rolled his eyes.

"He didn't kill him," Wyatt said settling on the sofa.

"Oh come on, Wyatt, I had him hook, line and sinker."

Jordan waved him off. "You think. I could tell you were lying."

"Yeah?" Billy asked taking out his knife and showing him the blood. "Then what's that?"

"Could have come from an animal."

"But it didn't."

"You two are full of shit."

"And you've got a dirty mouth, kid. I bet that's it. Your mom caught you jerking off to porn and you got all embarrassed and ran off."

"That's not it."

"Of course it was. That's what little dudes like you do."

"Shut up."

"Ooohh, we've got a tough guy here, Wyatt," Billy said tossing the remainder of his sandwich into the garbage and swigging some beer down. "You know he thinks this volcano is active."

Wyatt laughed.

"It is," Jordan said. "My mother is a volcanologist. Well she was one until she left the USGS and became an analyst at the University of Utah."

Billy glanced at Wyatt then frowned. "She's here with you?"

"Does it look like it?" he said in a sarcastic manner.

"I meant you're here with her."

"Was. Until she decided to head off and work with the USGS. She's all worried that Yellowstone is about to blow."

"Why?" Billy asked.

"Other than the earthquakes, all the fish are dead in the lake, and the animals are acting strange. Then there is the fissure down in Grand Teton National Park, and the drilling NASA is doing."

"NASA?"

"Yeah, I overheard them last night talking about NASA drilling down to release heat and inject water into the area around the magma. Something about cooling it down. I think it's all bullshit but my mother sure is fired up about it."

Billy looked over at Wyatt and thought about the boulders that had cut off the road through the canyon.

He recalled the steam and smoke pouring out of the earth. In all his years of coming to Yellowstone, he'd heard the rumors that it was going to blow. His uncle would talk about it at family reunions. He'd say that tourists were paranoid but it didn't stop them from showing up every year in droves. When asked what would happen if it did blow, he would take a sip of his whiskey and laugh. "It won't," he said. Maybe that's why he'd never really given it much weight. Perhaps that's why it didn't bother him to come back year after year to the park. In his mind there was more chance of being struck by an asteroid than the caldera erupting.

"So where is your mother now?"

"She dumped me with a tour group. A bunch of… 'Oh gee, dad, look at this steam coming out of the rock' type of people."

"Someone's jaded," Wyatt said before he laughed.

"Whatever, man. Anyway, I'm getting out of here," Jordan said rising to his feet. Billy walked over and pushed him back into the chair.

"You go when we say you do."

"What? You kidnapping me?"

Billy stared back at him and pursed his lips together. That's when the idea hit him. "Yeah. Yeah, we are."

"Billy," Wyatt said. "Can I have a word with you outside?"

Wyatt got up and headed out to the porch. Billy jabbed a finger at Jordan and sneered. "Stay put or else," he said shaking his rifle.

Outside he closed the door behind him. "Yeah?"

"Are you out of your goddamn mind?"

"What?"

"First you stab a ranger, now you want to kidnap a kid? Do you really want to spend the rest of your life behind bars?"

"Relax, dude. Think of him like our insurance policy." He stepped down off the porch. "To the north the road is blocked. If we go back we will run into roadblocks. That kid in there might be the only way we get out of this park."

"That kid has a mother who worked for the USGS, which I might add works with the national park. Don't you think right now they are looking for him?"

"Possibly. Kids go missing in this park all the time. They'll think he walked off."

Wyatt shook his head. "More like drove away. You heard what he said. They'll think he took the truck. Shit!" he yelled and crouched down wrapping both hands over his head as if he was going to rock back and forth like a mental patient.

"Calm down," Billy said.

"Calm down? This shit just keeps getting worse. I should have left you. Why did I come back?"

"Because you're my friend."

"No, because I'm stupid. I let you drag me around from park to park, jeopardizing my life, ruining my relationship with Rita, all for what? A few lousy bucks from sponsors."

"It's more than we were getting."

"Yeah, maybe, but at least then we weren't having law

enforcement chase our ass."

"Then what do you want us to do?"

"Leave him here, let's just go."

"They'll still be looking for us."

"Yeah but at least if we get found without him we won't get hit with a kidnapping charge."

Billy stared back and blew out his cheeks.

"You think there is any validity to what he's saying about the park?" Wyatt asked.

"No. This place hasn't erupted in thousands of years. A few earthquakes aren't a big deal. They have them all the time."

"Look, Billy, I think we should hang out here for a while at least until it gets dark. We can stash the truck in the forest for now just in case they do any flyovers and then head out this evening. Less chance of being seen."

"Yeah. Yeah, okay."

The odds were stacked against them and they weren't going to get out of the situation any quicker by hitting the road now. The best thing they could do would be to hide the truck and head out under the cover of darkness.

* * *

After touching down in Bridge Bay, Catherine met with two rangers and the family whose truck was missing. While they updated her, she looked out across the lake as fishermen tried to clear the lake and media people filmed segments for the news that night.

"I'm very sorry, Ms. Shaw. Sometimes there are just too many people to keep track of on these tours, that's why we usually like to have the parents come along."

"So you're blaming me?"

"No. No," Logan said stepping in. "I'll deal with this," he said to the ranger.

He led her away as she looked over her shoulder and scowled. She couldn't believe the nerve of them. "You hear that?"

"They're just doing their job, Catherine."

"Obviously not or my son would be here."

He lifted his baseball cap and ran a hand through his hair. "It's a little bit more complicated than that. Like I said earlier. They are already stretched. Usually a group of this size would have a few more rangers helping out but most of them are at checkpoints or out in the backcountry."

"What am I supposed to do?" she asked.

The park was massive. A missing person in Yellowstone National Park was like trying to find a needle in a haystack. It was sixty-three miles from north to south and fifty-four from east to west. It was full of canyons, alpine rivers, dense forest, hot springs and geysers and all manner of wildlife like bears, wolves, bison, elk and antelope. In many ways it was a modern-style jungle. And in the heat of summer it was the closest thing that the West could get to roaming the plains of Africa.

As they made their way back to a ranger's vehicle, Catherine felt the ground shake. It was subtle then stronger, and before she could turn to Logan, it stopped. They continued on, assuming it was just another tremor, but then heard people yelling. Both of them turned to see a large knot of visitors pointing to the forest on the east side of the lake. Smoke was rising. Logan snagged up his radio and tried to get in contact with one of the rangers.

"This is Logan Miller, what's going on?"

Static came over the radio before someone replied. "It's a forest fire."

Although some might panic, that wasn't Logan's first response. "Keep me updated."

"You don't seem too bothered?"

"Fires happen all the time, Catherine. Especially in the summer. They're a part of the ecosystem here in Yellowstone. Like earthquakes, we monitor them, sometimes we suppress them if we think they are a threat to human life and property but if there is no danger we often let a wildfire burn itself out. There are multiple ways we deal with natural fires."

"You don't think it's related to the caldera?"

"I hope not," he said opening the passenger side door on the ranger cruiser. Catherine was about to get in when she looked back at the lake. She squinted and cupped a hand over her eyes. Although she couldn't hear what was being said she could tell that something wasn't right. All the boats were making their way in and many of the people down at the dock were hurrying to get away from the lake itself.

Her eyes scanned the horizon and that's when she saw it.

A huge bulge forming in the lake. The waters rose sending a tidal wave towards the land, increasing in size with each passing second.

Chapter 17

If he hadn't seen it with his own eyes, he wasn't sure he would have believed it. Logan broke away from Catherine, dashing towards the lake, shouting to those unaware.

"Move it. Run!" he yelled. His eyes flitted between the crowd and the huge wave heading for shore. As rangers worked together to get people to safety, Logan spotted a tearful mother calling out to her kids. The poor woman was beside herself. He hurried over. "Ma'am, how many kids?"

"Two. My daughter is eight, blond and wearing a red outfit, and my son is ten. They were here a minute ago."

"Get back, I'll look."

He darted off into the crowd, frantically searching for anything that was red. It didn't take him long to spot the girl standing by herself crying her eyes out. "Mommy!" she yelled.

Logan barreled towards her and scooped her up. "Where's your brother?"

Through tears she told him that she couldn't find him. Logan scanned his field of vision for a few seconds but he had no other choice than to sprint away as the wave was nearly upon them.

As the crowd hurried away from the shore, it was like a stampede. People tripped and were trampled underfoot. The elderly, and those who couldn't move fast looked on in horror accepting their fate. It all happened in a matter of minutes. Logan looked back as he saw boats disappear below the wave, crushed by its power and weight. The color of the water looked different, almost a dirty brown, a stark difference from the clear waters that he was used to seeing.

The wave obliterated the dock, smashing it into pieces as the water spread inland. Those that were fast enough managed to escape into the surrounding forest. Logan looked back at the water as it washed into the parking lot, drowning people and lifting and swallowing vehicles like toy cars. All around him the sound of people's screams filled the air.

"Don't stop!" he yelled to those who stopped running to watch.

Carrying the young girl he raced deeper into the forest until the sound of water crashing behind them stopped. When he cast a glance over his shoulder for a third time, the water drew back into the lake. He could now see the extent of the devastation. Mangled bodies, crumpled cars, boats capsized, parts of the wooden dock scattered throughout the lot and signposts snapped like twigs. He put the girl down and she took off running. "Hey!"

Before he could get any further words out of his mouth the young girl's mother scooped her up, crying into the crook of her neck. The relief would be short-lived once she learned that her son was gone.

He cautiously walked towards the lot to get a better look. Crouching down where the asphalt met the grass, he touched the water left behind and brought it up to his nose. It smelled like sulfur. "Oh shit."

"Logan," Catherine cried out as she slipped through the crowd.

He turned as she ran over. "Come with me."

"Where we heading?"

"I want to see that fire."

They sprinted across what remained of the parking lot. It looked like a tsunami had ripped through the area. The marina buildings were destroyed, and in the distance they could see that the campsite hadn't been spared. Tents lay tattered, and RVs had been dragged and rolled. The lake had swept many to their deaths. Others had climbed trees. They jogged around the carnage and looked on at the horrified faces of those who'd survived until they came upon a ranger who had driven into the area to assist.

"I need to take your truck," Logan said to the ranger. "And get these people out of here."

"Send them where?" the confused ranger asked.

"North. We're putting this area of the park on evacuation notice."

"Evacuation?"

Logan couldn't say the entire park as he needed more information and right now they didn't have much to go on except a few abnormalities. There was a good chance that what they were witnessing was just the precursor. Within seconds they were peeling out of the campground heading around the lake on Highway 20.

Logan smashed the accelerator as they careened around a bend.

"Slow down," Catherine said.

He reached for his phone and tried to get a hold of Superintendent Harris but it just went to voicemail so he left a message.

"William, I need you to call me immediately. Hundreds of people are dead, the lake has flooded the mainland and the smell of sulfur is in the air. I need you to—"

The phone went dead and he looked at it. "Shit!" It needed charging. He tossed it on the seat.

"You can use mine." Catherine fished around in her jacket then looked back at him. "Oh man. It must have fallen out."

Logan smashed his fist against the steering wheel and accelerated hard heading towards the southeast. As they got closer they were able to get a clear picture of what was happening. On the east side of the road that circled the lake, a large portion of the forest was on fire. Ranger vehicles were turning back tourists who were trying to head that way. Logan drove around them turning on his lights so they wouldn't get stopped until he managed to get close to where the fire management team was shooting ropes of water into the forest and soaking the surrounding area to prevent flames from spreading. A wall of thick black-and-white smoke stretched across the landscape making it hard to see.

"Wait here," Logan said as he jumped out and went to the trunk and retrieved a mask to cover his face. Flakes of ash drifted past his field of vision as he jogged over to the fire crew who were doing their best to control the hellish fire. Fires were a common danger in Yellowstone. Most of them were started by lightning, and only a small percentage by humans.

"Where's the chief?" Logan asked a firefighter. He pointed to a guy barking orders. The firefighters were geared up in yellow jackets, dark pants, boots and white or yellow hardhats. They had formed a line and were raking the ground. A fire break was often created to act as a barrier to slow or stop wildfires. They would overturn the ground and cut through the undergrowth in the hopes of slowing or smothering the fire using the soil as a natural barrier.

The officer of fire management, otherwise known as the chief, was dishing out orders and overseeing the chaos when Logan approached. "You want to tell me what we've got here?"

"A nightmare." He bellowed out a few more orders to his men as if Logan wasn't even there before looking back at him. "What can I do for you?"

A gray and white coat of ash covered the landscape and the smoke had blocked out what little sun was in the sky.

"Any idea how this started?"

He knew there hadn't been any lightning or rain for the past few days, which meant either someone had started it, or something had. He was hoping, praying even, that the chief would tell him that a ranger had spotted kids playing with matches in the area but instead he shrugged. "No idea right now. We can't get close enough to even see what is going on. Whatever it is, it's bad as this is spreading fast and the wind isn't causing it."

"Who notified you?"

"A ranger by the name of Dawson." He pointed to a truck farther down.

Logan took off to get some more details. Although what had happened with the lake was enough justification to evacuate people within the surrounding area, he had to know what had caused the fire. If the caldera was responsible, that might give them enough proof to overturn the hesitation of his boss and the superintendent.

It was hard to see because of all the smoke. If he wasn't wearing the mask he wouldn't have been able to breathe.

He could hear the crackle of wood as tongues of fire spread across many acres of woodland consuming it like a disease. A column of smoke poured up above the forest billowing out and darkening the sky. Once Logan reached the ranger who was sitting in his truck he was out of breath. He placed a hand on the side of the truck and took a second to catch his breath.

"Dawson."

He turned, his face and ranger's outfit blackened by smoke. "Yeah?"

"You were the first on scene. Did you see what started it?"

He nodded. He looked as if he was just about to tell him when they heard a large explosion, and saw several firefighters running out of the forest, one of them covered in flames. He dropped and one of his colleagues threw a large silver blanket over him to extinguish the fire. The fire swirled and twisted devouring the trees and everything in its path.

Dawson looked on with a slack jaw.

Shock set in.

"Dawson. What did you see?"

"I... I was taking a group through the forest on a tour when the ground started shaking." He looked visibly shaken as he said it. He blew out his cheeks and inhaled deeply as if struggling to get air or reliving the moment in his mind. "The next second it split open. It happened so fast. Four hundred, maybe, five hundred foot fissure? It stretched across the forest floor then split wide, maybe fifteen feet." He wasn't even looking at Logan when he said it. "I tried to help them but it was too late. Some of the visitors lost their balance and fell into the gap. I..." He dropped his chin. No tears fell but shock had got the better of him. Logan placed a hand on his shoulder and thanked him. He waved over a couple medics and told them to get him out of there. He wasn't going to be of use to anyone in this state.

Armed with that new information he dashed back to the chief of fire and asked to use his phone. He tried again to get through to the superintendent but didn't have any luck.

"Damn it. Where are you?"

Catherine was patiently waiting for him when he returned. He ripped off the mask and hopped in, firing up the engine. The tires spun wildly as he reversed out and did a U-turn.

"What did you find out?"

"The earth split open. The heat from the ground. That's what caused this fire. We need to get back to Mammoth and have them contact the National Guard, and put the entire park on evacuation notice."

"I need to find my son."

Logan looked over at her as the truck roared down the highway. As much as he wanted to reassure her, he couldn't. The park was too vast and if this disaster had occurred here, what other tragedies had happened in the park? Overwhelmed by the situation he headed back to the campground and searched for another ranger to use their phone. Catherine told him he'd have more success trying to reach the USGS team. As long as they were aware of the situation they could handle it from there on out.

"You trust her?"

"She might be a bitch but there is one thing that she values more than anything else — her own life."

"No I mean, do you think she'd make the call?"

"She'll have to."

* * *

Ten minutes earlier, Rebecca had been talking to one of the lead scientists from NASA about the project to drill down and cool the area around the magma chamber. While she didn't make it clear to Catherine, she would have been lying to say she didn't have concerns surrounding the task.

It was touted as a three billion dollar project, and one that hadn't come about without scrutiny. Drilling into Yellowstone had been one of several dangerous solutions included in a report that she and higher-ups in the USGS had received several years ago. Even back then she thought it was a crazy idea. In her mind the potential for it to go wrong was huge. But unlike other projects she was involved in, this one was out of her hands. A year ago she'd learned the decision had been made by the NASA Advisory Council on Planetary Defense and as they got closer to the date of implementation they were told the park would be closed and communities in the area would be placed on alert.

None of that happened.

Since the proposal had been made, all talk of a date when drilling would commence went silent. Rebecca concluded that the idea had been scrapped.

It hadn't.

It was only when the increased activity of geysers in the park made headlines that she began to hear through the grapevine that NASA had decided to move ahead with the drilling project and had received the go-ahead from the president himself. Again, she assumed they would clear the park.

They didn't.

"Run that by me. Why hasn't the park been cleared?"

David Parkinson was the lead scientist heading up the project.

"It would have attracted too much media attention and then turned into a political fiasco and the president wanted to avoid that," David said.

"But you can't be sure that the events in the park aren't being caused by this drilling."

"It's highly unlikely. We haven't penetrated the magma chamber and there is only a small percentage that is actually molten lava inside. Seismic studies have shown us that it's mostly solid, made up of crystals that form as magma cools. So even if it did erupt we don't expect there to be any…"

Before he could finish what he was saying, the ground started to shake.

Rebecca latched on to one of her team members in front of her. She was inside a trailer that was being used as a command post. It was full of monitoring equipment and about eight NASA workers. David shot out of the trailer just in time to see the ground begin to crack.

People began yelling, and Rebecca moved across the trailer and hung on to a table, fearing for her life.

"Turn it off!" someone yelled. She couldn't tell if it was David or someone else.

Everyone inside that trailer hung on for dear life as the ground shook and the sound of rock splitting dominated. She had visions of the trailer being swallowed and her last moments on earth being burned alive.

No sooner had the earthquake started than it stopped and the only sounds that could be heard were men yelling outside and drilling. She glanced up at the seismic monitor and watched as the activity decreased, then increased, then dropped off again.

"What strength was it, Kyle?"

"5.2."

Rebecca moved quickly to the door telling them to follow her as she exited the trailer searching for David. That's when her phone started ringing. She glanced at the caller ID. She didn't recognize it but answered it.

"Rebecca, it's Catherine. I need you to listen to me."

Chapter 18

It was the stench of smoke carried on a northwest wind that reached them first. Billy was the first to notice. The sun had begun to wane behind the trees when Billy stepped outside to have a cigarette. They'd already stashed the truck in the forest and covered it to avoid being spotted. He'd promised the kid they would drop him off on their way out and that despite his animosity for his mother, it was best he stay with her. Despite all their flaws, and the initial idea to keep him as a form of insurance, they weren't assholes and they understood she was probably going out of her mind with worry at that very minute. Leaning against the porch post, Billy lit a cigarette and looked out at the final remnants of another July day. He lifted his nose and sniffed. At first he thought it was just cigarette smoke but then he noticed the faint glow of orange beyond the pines. "Hey, Wyatt."

"Yeah?" Wyatt said from inside the cabin.

"Come take a look at this."

Wyatt muttered something to Jordan and strolled out.

Billy gave a nod in the direction of the glow. "Does that look like fire to you?"

His eyes widened and Wyatt squinted then nodded.

"I'll get the truck. You get the kid."

He dropped his cigarette and stomped it out before moving at a quick pace away from the cabin. It wasn't uncommon to see fires in Yellowstone but he knew enough about wildfires to understand the threat. Wildfires were erratic. One minute they could be heading in one direction and then the next going in the other. It wasn't just the flames that were the problem, it was the smoke. More people died from smoke inhalation than being burned alive. A forested area like this was the worst place to be, and having only one or two routes out only added to the danger. It would be easy to become trapped.

Billy didn't bother dragging off the large fir tree branches covering the truck. He hopped inside and gunned the engine, tearing out of there and heading to collect Wyatt who was now outside with Jordan in his grasp.

He slammed the brakes on and Wyatt tossed Jordan in, and they tore away leaving a cloud of dust in their wake.

"What's going on?" Jordan asked.

"Shut up, kid," Billy said yanking the wheel hard to the left and leaving the wild meadow. The truck bounced onto a dirt trail. With the trail's northern passage cut off, they only had a few other options: go south and return to Highway 20 and hope to God that the checkpoint for the rangers was gone, go west and try to find a way through the forest, or attempt to find some way around the mountainous region. It wouldn't be easy as it was quickly becoming dark and some areas of the terrain were too dense for a truck, and too steep. Beads of sweat formed on Billy's brow as they headed back the way they came, hoping to go through Fishing Bridge and then north on Grand Loop Road.

"Billy. What if…?" Wyatt didn't need to finish what

he was saying. Billy twisted in his seat and reached for the rifle and handed it to him.

Chapter 19

Roads in every direction around Yellowstone Lake were clogged with traffic as fear turned into panic and survivors with working vehicles tried to evacuate the area. Logan honked the horn but it was pointless — he was boxed in on either side by bumper-to-bumper vehicles. Some of them had tried to go east but the lake's water had snapped trees and washed in capsized boats. Highway 20 was now blocked off, so drivers had taken Howard Eaton Trail, which cut through the western section of Yellowstone.

"We're not getting through here. Damn it!" Logan said. He got out of the vehicle while Catherine watched visitors do the same. Many left behind their vehicles and decided to hike out. Already Catherine could see on a small scale the lack of organization that existed. There was no plan; it was every man for himself.

Her conversation with Rebecca had gone better than

she thought it would.

Whatever hesitation she had before was now gone. She'd promised to contact the superintendent, update him on the latest changes and hope to God they could get the National Guard in to help with the fire soon.

"Logan!" she yelled but he couldn't hear her. Catherine unbuckled and got out. The glow of fire nearby lit up the night and a heavy smoke wafting across the lake was already making visibility low and breathing difficult. She coughed, and then covered her mouth with a handkerchief. Squinting into the blur of ghostly white smoke, Logan emerged holding a radio up to his mouth.

"Yes. We're on the north side of Yellowstone. And Tom, hurry."

With that said he pushed the radio back into its holster on the side of his belt.

"We've got a chopper coming."

"I thought you said you couldn't get hold of SAR."

"It's not them. It's a guy who works for the forestry service. He lives out in Cody. He has forward-looking infrared camera on the helicopter and will pick us up so we can do a sweep of the surrounding area. I figure if your son has taken that truck or someone else did and he's in it, they might be off the main roads, so there is a chance we'll spot them using FLIR."

"FLIR? With all this fire? Are you kidding me?"

"Listen, Catherine, it's the best option we have right now. In fact it's the only option. I can't guarantee we'll find him. If this gets any worse, we may have no other choice than to pull out."

"I won't leave my boy behind."

* * *

Several miles away, Billy slammed on the brakes as the headlights illuminated a huge fissure in the road. "Go that way!" Wyatt jabbed his finger to indicate the direction, telling him to drive parallel to the gaping break in the ground in the hope of finding an area where they could go around. The closer they got to the highway that encircled the lake the brighter the glow of fire became. Thick billowing smoke made it even darker than it actually was.

"I can't see a damn thing," Billy yelled before flicking on his high beams.

"Just keep going straight."

Billy glanced at Jordan. "Kid, you got a phone?"

"I did. Your buddy stomped on it."

"Are you kidding me?" Billy said, flashing Wyatt a glare.

"What? You wanted him to contact the law?"

"We could have used it."

"For what?"

Billy didn't bother to explain, the situation was getting direr by the minute and they were still a few miles from the exit to Highway 20. The truck bounced over the hilly terrain until Billy saw the fissure come to an end. He yanked the wheel a hard left and continued on. He squinted as the fire became visible and he suddenly realized the way through was blocked. "Shit!"

Veering away from the fire, he had no other choice than to head towards a dense forest. "Billy, what are you doing?"

"There's no other way through."

"But that's like a slalom obstacle course."

"You have a better idea?"

He knew if they could make it through, it would lead out to a large open area on the other side that fed down past Indian Pond, and came out on Highway 20. Billy eased off the brakes as they got closer to the tree line. It would slow them down but they had no other choice.

* * *

On the north side of Yellowstone, streams of specialized firefighters known as smokejumpers were making final preparations before being taken to a rendezvous point where aircraft would take them to battle the wildfire. Rebecca was waiting on the superintendent who was speaking with them before they left. After getting off the phone with Catherine she'd bundled the crew into the helicopter and headed back to Mammoth headquarters to speak with Harris.

After landing they hurried into the building with

Rebecca barking out questions.

"Mark, what are the readings now?"

"The seismic activity is rapidly increasing."

"Maria?"

"Across the board — sulfur emissions and thermal readings are off the charts."

She paced back and forth regretting not listening to Catherine. When Harris came in, she immediately launched into telling him what needed to be done. "We need to evacuate the park immediately."

"What? This is just a fire. We had several last year. I admit this one is a little out of control but..."

After bringing him up to date on the death of Hank, she continued. "This is not just a wildfire you are dealing with here. I just got off the phone with Catherine. Hundreds of visitors are dead after the lake flooded inland. There was a high amount of sulfur in the water. She also said that the fire was started after that last earthquake."

"Forgive me, but isn't this the same lady you said cried

wolf only a few years ago in California?"

"This information came directly from a ranger of yours. James Dawson."

"I'm familiar with him but…"

"Look, we are wasting time. I'll be the first to admit I've made mistakes in the past and I don't believe everything that comes out of Catherine's mouth, but on this… the evidence is as clear as day. The caldera is unstable and if we don't act now there is no telling what will happen."

"How sure are you?"

"Mark, care to fill him in?"

Mark began reeling off data regarding seismic activity, deformation and gas emissions and comparing it to what was seen prior to volcanoes erupting in other parts of the world. The look on Harris's face changed. He nodded several times and then leaned back on a table.

"And you think NASA's equipment is causing this?"

"One hundred percent. These kinds of readings we are getting don't happen overnight unless the caldera is provoked. Most eruptions happen after weeks, even months of heavy activity. This is occurring too fast. In essence, Mr. Harris, what NASA is doing could be likened to poking a wasp's nest. You can only do that so long before what's inside reacts."

"Have they stopped?" he asked.

"They've been told to but the USGS does not have the final say in what they do. This is out of our hands. You need to call the governor of Wyoming and issue a state of emergency. Maybe he can reason with them or contact the powers that be to halt the activity."

"And if they stop. What then?"

"There's no telling. Quite frankly it might be too late."

"Best- and worst-case scenario?"

"Best case — the eruption is small and the caldera doesn't fully unzip. Worst case, the whole thing goes up and we don't live to see tomorrow."

Rebecca knew that no one could say with confidence how much magma it would take to trigger a full eruption, and it was more likely a small eruption creating lava flows would happen than a giant explosion, but still... Thousands would die no matter how small the eruption, but if it was a smaller one, there was a greater chance of the surrounding states, and the whole country bouncing back. But the problem was there was no telling what would happen. All they could do was monitor the readings and prepare the park for a potential eruption.

Harris pursed his lips together and stared back at her. The color in his face vanished as he reached for a phone and made the call.

* * *

Billy expertly weaved around the trees as Wyatt guided him through.

"Well, one thing is for sure, whatever resources the park has out searching for us, they'll be throwing it at this fire. Maybe this is God's way of getting us out of this mess."

"When did you start believing in God?" Wyatt said.

"About ten minutes ago," he said before laughing. He looked at Jordan who looked scared. "Hey kid, tell me about California. Is it true it's full of sun and beach babes as far as the eye can see?" He didn't give two shits about California but he thought it would take his mind off the situation at hand.

"What?"

"California. What's it like?"

"Uh… it's alright. I guess."

"You guess?" Billy swerved at the last second to avoid a tree, and burst through bushes and over a rise. "Okay. Okay. So do you have a lady friend?"

He didn't reply to that.

"C'mon. What's she like?"

"Dark hair, green eyes."

"Yeah, what's her name?"

"Aliyah."

"Aliyah? That doesn't sound like a white gal's name."

"It isn't."

"So she's African American. Nice. Nothing like some cocoa butter."

"Billy," Wyatt said.

Billy shrugged. "What?"

Wyatt shook his head. "Watch out!"

Billy looked just in time and veered around a huge boulder.

"How about you keep your eyes ahead?" Wyatt said.

"What about you?" Jordan asked.

"What do you want to know?"

"What are you doing here in Yellowstone?"

He smiled as the truck bounced over the rocky terrain. "You ever heard of the Adrenaline Brothers?"

"Yeah. Two crazy guys who post videos online."

He laughed. "We've got a fan boy here."

Jordan looked at both of them. "No way. That's not you guys."

The truck soared over a rise and Billy yanked the wheel to the right. "In the flesh."

"Bullshit."

"Show him the bandanna." Wyatt pulled it from his backpack and flashed it.

"Anyone could have bought that."

"We don't sell the bandannas," he said pulling it out and showing him the logo on the front. Jordan gripped it in both hands and looked at it.

"No way."

"Unfortunately," Wyatt said looking out the side window as they burst out of the tree line into a large open field. In the distance they could see the lights of cars on the highway. Billy fist pumped the air and smiled. "And that's how you do it, ladies and gents."

The truck was roaring across the open plain heading for the road when the earth opened, one half rising five feet in the air and creating a wall before them. Billy swerved hard but not even he could avoid the collision. The side of the truck slammed into the earth, and the engine cut out.

He turned over the key as the earth began shaking. "C'mon!"

The truck spluttered a few times before it kicked in and he floored the gas pedal jerking them all forward. They had traveled on for another fifty yards when another portion of the earth blocked them. It felt like they were driving in a maze with walls appearing out of nowhere. Large clumps of soil rained down, smashing against the truck and blurring the window.

Wyatt leaned back, bracing himself as his mouth widened. "Watch out!"

Chapter 20

The powerful eruption shook the earth beneath them, toppling trees, and overturning vehicles. They were on the way to the helicopter rendezvous point in an open space called Bridge Creek not far from Howard Eaton Trail when a mushroom cloud of ash shot up into the air. In that instant there was no way to gauge the scope of the eruption, only that it had come from the lake far behind them. Even if it was only a small eruption, there was a possibility that it could destabilize the entire supervolcano. What followed was a series of quakes that tore the ground asunder. Like broken glass fissuring out, the ground spread throughout the park, the earth rose in some areas, and dropped in others, creating walls of soil and rock that were monolithic in size.

Dirt rained down in heavy chunks like balls of hail striking the hood and roof of their vehicle, beating out the rhythm of death.

Catherine glanced in the side mirror, her eyes widening in horror.

"Oh my God!" she muttered under her breath.

The SUV rocked from side to side, and trees collapsed around them.

It was a chaotic scene unfolding as vehicles disappeared into the ground, and large plumes of smoke, steam and ash shot into the air.

Logan didn't let up for a second but drove the gas pedal home, swerving around other vehicles until he veered off the main stretch heading for the coordinates Tom had given him.

"How long before he arrives?"

Logan glanced at his watch. It could be another ten minutes.

"We don't have that," she said. Logan skidded off the trail and over grass and slammed the brakes on. Both of them got out and looked back. A gust of hot wind blew at them bringing with it a thick wall of smoke. Flaked ash fluttered down and Logan ran to the back of the vehicle and grabbed out masks to cover their faces. He glanced at his watch and they looked to the sky. It was like being in a terrifying dream they couldn't escape. The glow of fire, mixed with the plume of ash, surrounded them. Catherine fully expected it to be scalding hot but it wasn't. Either the lake's water had cooled it or what had erupted was mostly steam, and solid material.

Several other vehicles must have seen their ranger's SUV pull off the main stretch because they followed. Two, then three, then about six vehicles came skidding in. Windows came down and a driver shouted, "What are you doing? Get the hell out of here."

Logan waved them on but they must have figured out why they were waiting as several of them got out and looked towards the sky.

"Shit," Logan said. If these people caught wind that they were waiting for a helicopter, a riot would ensue.

A man and his wife hurried over. "Are you waiting for search and rescue? Are they sending in helicopters?"

"Sir, get back in your vehicle and keep heading west."

"What are you doing out here? You're waiting for a ride out, aren't you?"

The man persisted until he grabbed hold of Logan.

"Sir, back up."

"We need to get out of here. We have kids."

Logan stabbed his finger. "Get in your vehicle and…"

An explosion of epic proportion shook the ground enough that all of them lost their balance. It sounded like a rocket igniting.

The man scrambled to his feet and grabbed his wife to hurry back to their vehicle. They didn't waste a second getting the hell out of there. Others in vehicles nearby followed suit.

"C'mon, Tom, where are you?" Logan said looking at his watch again.

Shock began to set in at the thought that Jordan was out there somewhere — lost, scared and liable to die if she didn't find him fast. How far could he have got? Catherine had to push down every emotion otherwise she would have lost it right there and buckled.

"Logan."

He wasn't looking at her but focused on the sky.

"Logan!"

"What?"

"If we don't make it out of this. I just wanted to thank you."

"For what"

"For trying."

She knew he could have just left her. He could have told her there was no point searching for her son but he didn't. He was risking his own life and his friend's life.

All the tension in his face disappeared for a second, and his lip curled before they heard the sweet sound of the chopper's blades thumping in the distance.

"All right. Listen up. As soon as we get on we'll do a couple of sweeps through areas where I think he might have gone but if we don't see him we are going to have to leave, you understand?"

Catherine nodded. This was all her fault. She shouldn't have left him behind. Hell, she shouldn't have brought him here. Inwardly she berated herself as the chopper emerged from the thick cloud and came down. Wind whipped at her clothes, as it got closer to touching down.

Right then three vehicles came barreling towards them.

"Logan!"

He pulled his firearm in preparation.

As the helicopter set down, Logan motioned for her to get in as he raked his gun in front of him. Drivers jumped out and bolted for the helicopter. She heard the crack of the gun, once, twice, then a third time before Logan hopped in and yelled at Tom.

"Get this bird in the air, now."

Chapter 21

The world came back into view in fragments, like a kaleidoscope of images. Foreign sounds bombarded his brain. Billy coughed hard, his eyes fluttering. He could hear someone speaking but couldn't make out who it was. He felt a warm trickle of something on his face. The taste of iron was in his mouth and it felt like someone was pressing down on his shoulders. Different sounds, crackling, popping and a brash voice dominated.

"Billy! Wake up!"

His eyes snapped open but he couldn't make sense of the world around him. He could smell burning plastic and hear it bubbling away. Slowly the memory of what just happened came back to him, and he realized he was hanging upside down, with his shoulders against the top of the truck. He was still buckled into his seat and Wyatt was trying desperately to get him out.

He saw flames outside, and the kid beside him still

strapped in but unconscious.

"The truck's on fire," Wyatt said. "Where did you put your knife?"

He reached to his side but the blade wasn't in the sheath. He groaned in pain. It felt like he'd broken a rib or two. Wyatt began looking around for the knife. He was panicking. Beyond the truck, Billy couldn't see much, just fire, and soil and hissing steam. The last memory he had was of yanking the wheel hard as large sections of the earth rose up before them. It had all happened so suddenly.

"Found it."

Wyatt scrambled over and began hacking away at the seatbelt until his body jerked free. Wyatt looped his arms around Billy and dragged him out through the passenger side window. He brought him about fifty yards from the truck, then collapsed on the ground.

In that moment all he could hear was the fire crackling away.

Both of them breathed hard as they tried to catch their

breaths.

"The kid," Billy muttered, motioning to the truck.

Wyatt shook his head. "There's not enough time."

Billy grabbed him by the collar. "Get the kid out."

"But." Wyatt stared back, fear ruling his every thought. Reluctantly he nodded and hurried away. Billy rolled onto his side to watch but had to move to his back, as it was just too painful. He gripped his side and let out a cry. It had been one bad thing after another. Although he wasn't a churchgoing man he knew the danger of the situation and the need for some divine intervention.

"God. If you are out there, please help us."

In the few minutes he was waiting for Wyatt, he thought about his mother who had passed away when he was nine years old. She'd been a churchgoing woman, and someone who didn't mince words when it came to spirituality. Was there any validity to it? He didn't know as he'd lost his faith after she died. But was it really lost? Another explosion and he felt the ground shake. It was like lying on a vibrating bed in a sleazy motel. Within minutes, Wyatt returned with the kid in his arms. He was out cold. He laid him down and Wyatt checked his pulse and put his ear up to his mouth. "He's alive," Wyatt said.

Suddenly the truck exploded, and both of them looked back shielding their eyes from the intense glare of the flames.

"You've got quite a gash on your chin, Billy. Can you walk?" Wyatt asked.

It took him a minute or two to feel confident to sit up, as he was still feeling sick to his stomach, dizzy and unsure of what bones he might have broken. He motioned to Wyatt who helped him up. Back on his feet he grabbed his left side. He'd definitely broken at least one rib, maybe two. He hobbled for a second until he found his feet.

"Okay, I'm good."

"You sure?"

"Yeah."

Another shake, this time of epic proportion. And this time it wasn't from the truck. In the distance, beyond the forest they saw a mushroom cloud of gray smoke rise into the atmosphere.

"Holy shit," Billy said.

"Look, we've got to get out of here. Let's go." Wyatt tried to pull him away.

Billy gave a nod to Jordan. "What about the kid?"

"He'll slow us down. There's nothing we can do for him."

"There was a first-aid kit back at the ranger cabin."

Wyatt walked back to him. "Are you out of your mind? We are not going back there. That's several miles from here. We'll be lucky to make it out of here alive."

"There was a radio there."

Wyatt frowned. "What?"

"Yeah, in the rear of the cabin. It was covered up with a sheet. Looks old but it might work."

"And it might get us killed. No, I say we go now. Maybe we can get to Fishing Bridge and catch a ride with someone before…"

Another explosion and the earth shook even harder.

Huge boulders broke away from steep slopes nearby and barreled down slamming into trees like bowling pins. Before they were able to make a decision, Jordan started coughing. Billy made his way over and crouched down. "Hey kid, you okay?"

It took him a second to realize where he was, and then he nodded.

"Come on, let's get you out of here."

Billy turned to head northeast when Wyatt came running over. "Billy. Billy."

"Look behind you, Wyatt. We aren't getting down to Fishing Bridge, it's cut off, and the caldera is exploding in that area and we have no transportation to get us out of here. Our best bet is to head back to the cabin and try that radio, and hope to God search and rescue finds us." Wyatt attempted to argue. He suggested they head north but it was too risky as it would take them up to a higher elevation and he didn't think he could make it that far. Billy was sure he was suffering from internal bleeding. The pain was excruciating with every breath he took.

"Screw it," Billy said. He helped Jordan up and they began the trek away from the wildfire and explosions. He wasn't an idiot. He knew the chance of them getting out of this mess was slim but after all he'd done in his life, if it ended here, he was willing to accept that. Wyatt cursed under his breath as he looked back at the burning truck and the glow that was getting closer by the second.

Chapter 22

"I can't have this bird in the air long," Tom yelled as the helicopter swooped over the vast ocean of trees. Now they were up, Catherine could see the size of the devastation. Thousands of acres had already been turned into a blazing furnace by the initial fire just west of the lake, and since the last explosion, the wind was forcing it north of Fishing Bridge. But that wasn't the worst threat. Her eyes widened as she saw where the eruption had occurred. The water in the lake was no longer there, in its place was hot lava spewing out, overflowing in every direction and moving outward, destroying everything in its path. Though devastating to see, it was clearly a small eruption compared to what could have happened. Still they weren't out of the woods yet. If an eruption had started here, where in the park might another occur?

"Tom, what are we getting on the FLIR?" Logan asked.

"See for yourself," he said moving the device around so he could look at the screen. FLIR, which was short for forward-looking infrared allowed them to see anything that emitted heat. But it wasn't just heat it detected, it could pick up small differences and display them as shades of gray in black and white.

"How do you make sense of that? I mean tell the difference between the fire and people down there?"

Tom veered the helicopter to the left. "Everything gives off thermal energy including cold objects. But the hotter something is the more energy it emits. We call it a 'heat signature'. Even if two objects are close together and both have different heat signatures they will show up clearly on the FLIR. You see that," he said pointing to what appeared to be a crowd of ants moving along. "Those are people. And that over there is a vehicle, and the rest is wildlife." He exhaled hard. "All this ash rising into the air is going to affect the blades. Where am I going, Logan?"

Logan gave him directions and Tom shot him a

concerned look.

"That's where this eruption is boiling over."

"It's also where they might have gone. The east would have been the closest way out of the forest."

"And what if they went west?"

"Then let's take a look."

The drone of the rotor blades was almost hypnotic. Outside the thin windows they could barely see where they were going. It was like they were in a snowstorm, except it wasn't snow falling.

"You said it was a black truck?"

"Yeah," Logan replied.

"There are countless black trucks out here. I'm gonna need something more specific than that."

"Look, just take it back around one more time over to the east side and if we can't see anything we'll head out."

Catherine leaned forward from the back and slapped Logan on the arm.

"I'm sorry, Catherine. But Tom's right. We are already risking our lives being up here. These birds can't handle these kinds of conditions."

Catherine placed her head in her hands and began to weep. Her son meant everything to her. It had nearly destroyed her when she lost him in a custody battle and then to see how his father had turned him against her was even more heartbreaking, but if she survived this and he didn't, she wouldn't be able to live with herself.

She looked out towards the plume of ash stretched across miles of landscape. Tom flew the helicopter around the eruption site, keeping a good distance. The rhythmic thump of the blades was steady as it displaced smoke all around them.

Far below the fire had burned its way through the forest leaving nothing but scorching hot ash. The flames crept forward in every direction. Where there was once a lake, thick lava, mud and debris flowed out rolling over everything in their path and consuming it. To the north it was dark, not even the glow of a fire could be seen, leading Catherine to believe that the USGS team were still alive and functioning. Had Rebecca followed her instructions? Had the superintendent called the Wyoming National Guard to assist in the evacuation? As it stood it no longer mattered. She looked out into the darkness then back at the FLIR camera.

"Anything?"

"Nothing. Just the wildfire," Logan said. "Tom, we'll circle back around one more time but…"

"Wait. What's that?" Catherine said pointing to a heat signature that seemed out of place from the inferno that was marching across the landscape like an army. Tom looked and nodded. "Looks like we've got something down there."

"Could just be a crashed vehicle," he replied.

"Bring it down, Tom."

"Roger that."

Tom flew the helicopter through a cloud of debris, skimming the tops of subalpine trees until the landscape opened up and he brought it down on a flat area a short distance away from where the earth had cracked open. Out the window, Catherine could see a truck had turned over on its side. He steadied the helicopter until they felt it bounce slightly on the earth.

"Don't be long," Tom yelled.

Logan and Catherine hopped out and double-timed it over to the fiery wreckage. Catherine was beside herself with worry. The thought of Jordan being inside made her shake. More explosions erupted from off in the distance. It was like being in a war zone.

"You see anything?"

Logan raised an arm and tried to get close but the heat coming from the truck was too much. All they could make out was the charred steel bones, and flames licking up inside, eating the truck up.

"I don't see him but that's the truck."

Logan had pulled out a pad of paper and was comparing numbers. He pointed to the license plate that was barely intact. Paint was bubbling and dripping, and the windows were smashed.

"Maybe he got out."

Logan stood there shaking his head, looking at the

torn earth, and all the fire blazing away.

"Catherine, we don't know if he was even in the truck. For all we know it could have been someone in the park who took the vehicle for a joyride."

"No. My boy's alive. I can feel it in my gut."

* * *

Wyatt was the first to burst through the door of the cabin. The other two stumbled in after him, out of breath and in pain. Although Jordan had been unconscious the longest, he appeared to have scraped through it with just a few cuts and bruises. Billy hadn't been so lucky. The pain in his stomach had intensified leading him to believe that he was suffering some form of internal bleeding from smashing into the steering wheel.

"Where is it?" Wyatt asked.

Billy threw up a hand and Jordan assisted him in taking a seat.

Wyatt shot into the rear room and threw off the sheet. He pulled out the flashlight Billy had given and shone it over the aged ham radio. It was a piece of junk. Wyatt ran his hand over a thick layer of dust searching for the on switch. He'd never used one before but how hard could it be? He figured it had to be tuned into a frequency that all the rangers were on, wouldn't it?

"Any luck?" Billy asked.

"I'm looking for the plug."

He dove under the table and batted cobwebs out of his face until he found a plug. He jammed it into the wall, hope filling his being as he came up to find the on switch. He must have tapped every button until a light blinked on. It lit up like a Christmas tree, and a faint static came over the receiver.

"Oh sweet God, thank you!" He scooped up the black microphone and tried to get someone. "Hello. Hello. Come in. Can anyone hear me?" He released the button but nothing came back except static. He turned several knobs, each time repeating himself.

"Come in. Mayday. Mayday. If you can hear this we are northeast of Yellowstone Lake in a ranger's cabin. We have an injured ranger. Come in. We have an injured ranger."

He glanced back and Billy gave him the thumbs-up. He knew they wouldn't respond unless it was one of their own but then again under the circumstances was anyone left in the park?

A sudden tremor began, and the entire cabin shook. Outside a portion of the porch collapsed and Billy yelled for him to hurry up.

Chapter 23

On the north side of Yellowstone, efforts were already underway to evacuate visitors in the park. It was a monumental task that would no doubt draw a lot of critics after the event. However, little thought was being given at that moment to the consequences or backlash from the public. That would come in time. As it stood, getting the word out was every bit as hard as Harris believed it would be. The ten visitor centers, and seven ranger stations throughout the park had been notified by radio, and instructed to alert visitors in the twelve campgrounds. It wasn't that he didn't think they would be unaware, the earthquakes throughout the day and eventually the mushroom cloud looming over the park had already forced people into escaping, but they couldn't leave anything to chance. The political fallout would be horrendous if he didn't ensure that he had done everything within his power to get people out.

His staff and the rangers were told that if they left now he would understand but their assistance wouldn't be overlooked. The National Guard had been notified and he'd been reassured they would be on hand to help. When they would arrive was another thing entirely. Harris stood with the USGS team looking up at a TV as the governor of Wyoming issued a state of emergency. Every few minutes the ground would shake, the tables would clatter and the doors would rattle.

Rebecca had stepped out to their van to monitor activity. She was waiting on a phone call from Catherine to let her know they were on the helicopter.

Mark leaned forward and looked at one of the four computers they had for monitoring recent activity in the park. "That seismic swarm is increasing. Those periodic bursts of gases are steady and the temperature is rising." He turned in his seat. "It's not slowing down, Rebecca."

"Ms. Lyons. A word," Harris said looking nervously out across the parking lot. Rebecca rose from her seat in the back of the van, ducked her head and stepped out.

"NASA has stopped drilling."

"Across all drill sites?"

"As far as I know."

There were three sites.

"I'm afraid it's too late," Rebecca said.

"What do you mean?"

"The damage is already done." She glanced out at the giant plume of gray ash that continued to rise and spread, making the evening really dark. "Look, there is a very good chance we will survive this. However the death toll will still be high."

"But I thought you said this is a minor eruption."

"It is. Listen, the eruption over Yellowstone Lake is huge, though minor compared to what could happen, or may still happen."

"May still happen? You're suggesting this could get worse?"

"We don't have a road map for how this volcano will react. Best-case scenario, this goes no further than the park, worst case, it continues to erupt until the whole caldera unzips."

"And if it does?"

"It will throw us into a situation like the kind after the eruption of Mount Tambora." She returned to the van with Harris in her shadow.

"Mount Tambora?"

"The following year became known as the Year Without Summer because of the severe climate abnormalities that caused temperatures to decrease across the northern hemisphere." She turned around as she stepped into the van. "Which means, a whole lot of people would die."

"Well let's hope to God that doesn't happen." He hopped in and came up behind them and looked over their shoulders as they continued to monitor the activity. "Where is Ms. Shaw?"

Mark pointed on the map to the heart of Yellowstone where swarms of earthquakes were building in intensity. "The last earthquake was an M6.4."

Rebecca scooped up the radio and stepped back out just as another explosion shook the ground, this time it caused the Albright Visitor Center and Museum's windows to smash, and a portion of it to collapse on the west side. Multiple lampposts sank into the ground as if some invisible force was pulling them down, and a huge section of the road disappeared causing a massive sinkhole.

"Mark, grab whatever equipment we have now and let's get the hell out of here."

"But what about Catherine?"

Rebecca got on the radio in the hopes of reaching Logan.

"Come in, Logan."

There was a slight delay before he replied.

"Go ahead," Logan replied.

"How far are you from Mammoth?"

"We're still looking for Catherine's son."

"No. Listen, Logan, you need to get out of there now. There's no time. Based on our readings this isn't going to get any better."

Another sudden shake was so forceful that it took her feet out from underneath her and caused Rebecca to fall against the truck. Fear shot through her, her pulse sped up and her forehead broke out in beads of sweat.

"Rebecca!" Logan yelled over the radio. "Come in."

Breathing hard and still gripping the truck she looked down the road at the large fissure that had opened up. A deep red glow emanated from inside as steam pushed up like dragon's breath, full of fire and sulfur.

"Tell Catherine I'm sorry. We've got to go," Rebecca said.

With that said she ended the communication and tossed the radio inside the truck. "Mark, go tell the rest of the team we are leaving now."

He hopped out and sprinted into the building.

She turned to say something to Harris only to see him lying lifeless on the asphalt. Large chunks of concrete from buildings nearby had crumbled and toppled down crushing him, as he tried to flee.

Rebecca hurried to the front of the van, slid through a gap that separated the back from the front and fired up the engine. Ahead of her, vehicles peeled out at rapid speeds, and park workers and visitors frantically ran to vehicles, some of which were now overturned.

She glanced behind her and saw the readings on the computers. All of them were off the charts. "C'mon. C'mon," she muttered waiting for the others to come out.

Another shake.

This time it was even stronger than the last.

The entire van shifted to the left as the asphalt began to melt. She threw the gear into drive and peeled away trying to dodge the cracks in the ground. Behind her she thought she heard Mark yell, "Rebecca, come back." But she didn't look to see if it was him. Fear drove her on; self-preservation was all that mattered now.

A large post came crashing down across Stable Street and tore through Yellowstone Federal Credit Union blocking her way out. She backed up and then saw her team running down the road trying to catch up. Turning the vehicle she pulled onto Canteen Road and drove halfway down the road when guilt kicked in. She slammed on the brakes and all the equipment in the rear flew off the counters and clattered across the floor. Waiting for the team she watched as the ground opened in areas and hydrothermal steam shot in the air burning people alive.

The suspension on the truck dropped and bounced as one by one the team launched themselves into the back.

"What the hell is wrong with you? Did you not hear me?" Mark shouted.

She shook her head.

"Go!" Maria yelled.

Rebecca slammed her foot against the accelerator and took off.

* * *

The heavy ash beat against the window making it almost impossible to see. The usually clear, steady sound of the helicopter blades was now muddled by the onslaught of smoke, debris and ash. Tom was doing his best to navigate through low visibility and provide one final sweep of the area before they pulled out.

"Where would you go?" Catherine kept saying over and over as if trying to know her son, and what he might do in this situation. Tom leaned over and muttered the words Logan knew were coming. He nodded and twisted around.

"Catherine. We need to pull out now. We don't want to get low on fuel and if we don't leave now this ash is going to bring us down." She sat there shaking her head unable to grasp that her son was lost.

"Where would you go?" she said turning to Logan. "The mountains or the east?"

He turned back and looked out the window, racking his brain. That's when someone came over the radio. "Come in. Come in. Anyone." Tom looked over at Logan.

"We read you loud and clear. Who is this?"

"We are trapped at a ranger's station, or cabin just northeast of the lake. We need help. We have an injured ranger."

"Ask him if Jordan is there. Ask him!" Catherine said leaning forward in her seat.

Tom posed the question and they waited for an answer. It never came. "Come in. Can you hear me?" Tom yelled.

There was no response.

"I know where that cabin is," Logan said. "Turn the bird around, Tom. It's less than two miles from here."

Tom shook his head. "Logan."

"Just do it. I'm not leaving a ranger behind."

Chapter 24

Outside the cabin, devilish flames seeped through bulges and cracks in the ground. An earth-shattering quake rocked the area and tore the earth apart. Billy gripped his ribs and looked out at what remained of the porch. Most of it had disappeared into the ground.

"It's not working," Wyatt yelled. "C'mon!"

"I thought you were in contact. I heard them," Billy replied.

"The damn thing isn't working. Come in. Can anyone hear us?" he yelled over the noise of the tremors.

Billy turned to his friend. "Wyatt, we need to leave now."

Jordan was gripping the kitchen counter, his eyes bulging as every few seconds the earth would move violently beneath them. Wyatt slammed the microphone down and swiped the whole unit onto the ground. "Damn thing!"

It was like the whole landscape was alive as the tectonic plates moved beneath. It felt like they were standing on watery ground. The floor of the cabin would move and rock and then settle for a few seconds before doing the same again.

Billy was about to step out when the whole ground crumbled, and the yard divided. A wall of steam shot up forcing Billy back into the house. Another quake tore away at the house and what remained of the porch caught on fire.

"Shit! Go. Out the back," Billy yelled.

They hurried towards the rear and flung the door open only to find a gaping gash in the earth full of fire and smoke. Billy started coughing as thick sulfuric smoke drifted into the cabin making it hard to breathe. Their eyes stung and the heat was becoming unbearable.

"What now?" Wyatt hollered.

Billy hurried to the east side of the cabin and looked out the window but they were cut off. The earth had crumbled around them and pulled apart, leaving a fiery moat. He sprinted over to the west only to find a wall of soil slammed up against the window. Slowly he backed up shaking his head.

"Billy. Billy!" Wyatt said.

He flung up a hand. "Shut up. Let me think."

His mind was spinning frantically but nothing came to him. They only had two options. One was to attempt a jump over a ten-foot gap with hot hydrothermal steam shooting out. The other was to climb up onto the top of the house and wait until it collapsed and hope to God that the house shifted sideways to form some kind of bridge. Neither of the options were good.

"Up," Billy said. "Get up on the roof."

"What?"

"You want to jump. Be my guest," he said motioning to the rear and front doors. Not wasting another second Wyatt climbed out the window on the east side, moved over carefully and launched himself onto the drainpipe.

"C'mon, kid, you're next," Billy said.

He shook his head and took a few steps back. "I can't

do it."

"Yes you can."

"I can't."

"Listen, you don't have another choice. It's either up or down."

Tears streaked Jordan's face and his hands shook. Outside Wyatt yelled to them to hurry up. More explosions erupted and trees disappeared into the earth in a steaming plume of smoke. Billy got in front of Jordan and grabbed him by both arms.

"Kid. It's okay to be afraid. Do you know after all these years of filming these insane videos, both of us still shit ourselves when we step up the edge of a mountain and jump off?"

Jordan looked up at him. "Really?"

"Every time. The only difference between you and me is that I refuse to let fear control me. Now get your ass out that window."

Jordan nodded and cautiously moved towards the window just as another eruption shook the house causing the floor to tilt sideways, and some of the planks to explode. Splinters of wood shot in every direction as Billy coaxed Jordan out to where Wyatt was ready to grab his hand and pull him up.

"You got him, Wyatt?"

"Yep!"

Jordan disappeared in front of him and Billy made his way out. He stumbled in pain, gripping his side again. This time he lifted up his shirt and could see half of his body had turned purple and black. He coughed and blood splatter came out of his mouth. "Fuck!"

He climbed out and made his way onto the roof. He coughed again.

As soon as he was up he could see the extent of their situation.

It was bad.

For miles around them the earth had morphed into a hellish nightmare. The glow of red lines fissuring out illuminated the night. Steam shot up, and smoke made the air thick, humid and almost unbreathable. Jordan coughed and Billy reached into Wyatt's backpack and pulled out one of their bandannas. He handed it to him and Jordan wrapped it around his face.

"Now what?" Wyatt said.

Billy looked up into the night sky, as dark clouds formed overhead.

"Let's hope he's listening."

The house shook again and Wyatt stumbled back and rolled down the roof. Billy launched himself forward, grabbing his leg just at the last second before he went over. One hand clung to a small vent on top and the other held on to Wyatt for dear life. Wyatt hung upside down. "Don't let me go."

"I won't. Jordan!"

Jordan scrambled down on his butt to help. He latched on to Wyatt's other leg and together they pulled him back up. All three of them climbed up to the ridge and looked out as lava and flames seeped out through voids in the ground, devouring everything in their path. Even if they could have jumped that gap, where could they have gone? Newly formed fumaroles ejected boiling water into the air. The steady sound of hissing and whistling mixed with the crackle of flames was beyond unnerving — it was terrifying.

The cabin shifted violently again and Billy clung tight, resigned to his fate.

"Wyatt. I'm sorry for bringing you here, man."

"Shut up. I chose to come."

"No, I pestered you. Rita was right. You should have given up this gig a year ago."

He reached into his pocket and pulled out a pack of smokes and handed him one. Jordan went to take one and Billy pulled it away. "Sorry, kid, not this time."

They lit up and stared out.

"Man, if we could have got this on video. Can you imagine how many views we would have got?"

Wyatt chuckled. "We would have gone to number one in trending videos."

They briefly laughed before their smiles disappeared.

"It's been a wild ride, my friend."

"That it has."

Another shake and Billy dropped his cigarette. "Damn it."

"You can have mine," Wyatt said. "I should have given up that shit a long time ago."

"Hold on, did you hear that?" Jordan said.

"The sound of death? Yeah, I heard it, kid," Billy said before taking a large drag on the cigarette.

"No. Listen." Jordan stood up and squinted into the dark smoke that billowed around them.

Wyatt cupped a hand to his ear while Billy laid back and looked up into the night sky. The next thing he felt was Wyatt tapping his leg. "Billy. Billy."

He looked up as a helicopter burst through the smoke.

"Hey! Hey," Wyatt shouted, as he and Jordan began waving their arms.

The steady thump of its blades roared loudly, and wind whipped at their clothes the closer it got. The helicopter passed over them and circled back around, this time slowing down. The door on the side of the helicopter opened and a law enforcement ranger came into view. He reached for a steel mesh rescue basket and unhooked a latch. A heavy-duty cable attached to the basket began to lower. It made a whirring sound as it came down. The ranger shouted for them to put Jordan in it. It could only take one person at a time.

"Remember what I said, kid," Billy said as Jordan cautiously climbed inside it.

The noise of the helicopter was deafening.

Whump. Whump. Whump.

It retracted up and within seconds they had him inside.

"You're next," Billy said thumbing up.

"No. You go, this place is about to drop."

Billy smirked. "Get your ass up there now. I'll be right behind you."

They looked up waiting for the ranger to emerge.

Another explosion and this time the cabin shifted hard to the left. Billy and Wyatt dove for the ridge as the foundation began to burn. Flames began to eat through the main cabin.

"Come on!" Wyatt yelled.

The ranger looked out and was yelling something as the mesh basket lowered. Wyatt couldn't hear him but Billy did.

"It can only take one person," Billy said.

"What?"

"Get on it."

"No. We both go or none of us do."

"Listen, you stubborn asshole, chances are I'm not going to make it anyway." He pulled up his shirt and showed him the damage to his ribs as he breathed heavily.

Wyatt stared and shook his head. "No, we'll get you to the hospital."

"You don't get it, brother. That bird up there can only carry so much weight."

"Bullshit. It's going to have to carry you too."

Billy smiled. "You've got two kids and one on the way. Get up there."

"I'm not going."

Another shake and both of them clung tightly, fear now getting the best of them.

Wyatt stared back at him before waving off the ranger.

"What are you doing?" Billy asked.

"You go down so do I. It's always been us."

"Stubborn asshole." He sighed. "Okay. Let's go."

They scrambled over to the basket and Billy told Wyatt to get in and he would hold on to the cable as it went up.

"It can't carry both of you," the ranger yelled.

Another explosion and the cabin shifted again.

"What did he say?" Wyatt yelled.

"He said…" Billy smiled. "I'll see you on the other side."

Billy gave the ranger the thumbs-up and hopped off the basket. It shot up and Wyatt leaned over desperately reaching down. "NO!"

It was too late. Billy looked up at him. Within seconds, the cabin gave way and Billy and the roof vanished into a gaping hole full of tongues of fire. The helicopter flew away, exploding out of the smoke as Wyatt stared back, his heart now in his throat.

* * *

High above the treetops of Yellowstone, the four-seater Robinson R44 helicopter soared east over the scorched park heading for Cody so Tom could refuel. With the addition of the tearful stranger on board, it was carrying beyond the maximum weight allowance. Catherine clung to Jordan and ran a hand down his blackened face. Logan briefly asked the stranger what happened to the ranger but he just shook his head.

"His name's Wyatt," Jordan said.

Wyatt looked at him but said nothing. Few words were exchanged on the journey out of the park as all of them were in shock. Catherine stared out the window, grateful to have her son back in her arms and yet still concerned that the worst of it wasn't over.

Heavy flakes of ash fell like snow smothering the park like a gray blanket.

Fortunately, four hours after refueling in Cody and

continuing their journey east, her fears were soon relieved when the USGS team made contact and updated her on the situation. The conversation with Mark was brief and to the point as Rebecca was in no frame of mind to speak. "Over the past hour, quake frequency in Yellowstone has dropped off. Gas emissions are still high but we're not getting the level of seismic activity as before. I'm not saying we're out of the woods yet, but what we are seeing from the data is positive. It looks as if this was just a small eruption. Not the full thing. We'll continue to monitor it closely over the next seventy-two hours."

"What was the magnitude of the last one?"

"An M7.7. But like I said, the swarm has decreased and the last three have been 2.8, 2.1 and 1.6. Had it been over 8, I think we would have been looking at a full eruption. As it stands, we might have got lucky."

"You think NASA might have contributed to that?"

Mark chuckled. "In more ways than one."

Catherine nodded and looked out. "Where are you now?"

"In the air. We made it out of the park and headed to Billings to catch a private flight east. We'll be working out of Maine if you want to join us there. What about you?"

"On our way to New York. Any update on the death toll?"

"Not so far. We'll know in the coming week."

"Thanks, Mark."

"Look, Catherine, for what it's worth I didn't doubt you, and had I been in charge maybe this would have played out differently."

"I appreciate that." She breathed in deeply. "What about Rebecca?"

"Yeah, she's in a bad state. She's already handed in her resignation. She wanted me to pass on her apologies."

"A little late for that now."

"I know."

Silence stretched between them for a minute or two.

"Maybe you should apply for her position."

"Me?" Mark asked.

"You're the best they have, Mark. And with Rebecca

gone, they are going to need someone strong at the helm.
"

"We'll see," he said. "Look, stay safe and we'll speak later."

After she got off the radio she walked back inside to join Logan, Jordan and Tom who were sitting in the lounge of a private airport just outside of Minneapolis.

Epilogue

TWO YEARS LATER

The late September sun smiled warmly over the vast crowd gathered in Mammoth, Wyoming. Among the numerous people, Catherine, Jordan, Logan, Wyatt, Tom and Hayden stood outside the newly rebuilt Albright Visitor Center and Museum for a tree planting ceremony to commemorate the dead. Six thousand, four hundred and twenty-two visitors and workers died in the initial eruption, and another three thousand and seventy-eight from the volcanic ash fallout that spread further afield. Though extremely high in number, the toll was only a fraction of what it could have been had it been a full eruption. Yellowstone had once again demonstrated its power, and its unpredictability. While over the past few years researchers and analysts had gathered at conferences to discuss the likelihood of another eruption, most were focused on learning from the past event. NASA and the

USGS took the brunt of the criticism, as news and chat shows around the country pointed fingers and tried to turn it into something more than it was.

Survivors from across the globe stood shoulder to shoulder as a sign of strength as the new superintendent, Michelle Douglas, thanked the newly appointed USGS scientist-in-charge Mark Bowman. He'd just finished giving a speech to discuss the lessons learned, and new technology they were working on to prevent a tragedy like this from happening ever again.

"Thank you, Mr. Bowman," Michelle said. "As all of you know, today is for us a bittersweet moment. While we will never forget the mistakes of the past, we learn and grow stronger because of them. However, that isn't the reason why we are gathered here. We are here today to remember those who lost their lives, to celebrate who they were, who they could have been and to find comfort in each other. And let us never forget those who sacrificed themselves to save others." She paused. "So, it's with great joy that I get to unveil the plaque with the names of the fallen." She stepped to her right and pulled away a white sheet that was attached to a commemorative wall near the visitor center. Behind it a gleaming bronze plaque had the inscriptions of thousands of names. There was a huge round of applause and then two minutes of silence followed.

When the ceremony was over and the crowds began to thin out, Catherine told Logan and Tom she'd join them for coffee in a few minutes. Jordan had something he wanted to do first.

She watched from a distance as her son walked over to one of the many trees they had planted that day. He stared down at it and removed a bandanna from around his wrist and tied it off around the Douglas fir. Wyatt walked over and placed a hand on his shoulder. "I think Billy would have appreciated that."

"You think so?"

"Yeah." Wyatt took a deep breath. "Kid, thank you for not saying anything to law enforcement. My family…" he trailed off.

Jordan smiled and looked back down at the tree.

"Look, if you and your mom are ever in Maine, you make sure you drop by, okay? Here's my address." Wyatt fished into his pocket and then gave him a scrap of paper. "I'd like to show you some of the footage that we recorded that was never uploaded."

Jordan stared at the scrap of paper. "I'd like that to see that."

Wyatt ruffled his hair. "Well I should get back. It's a long journey home."

He turned to walk away.

"Wyatt," Jordan said casting a glance back.

"Yeah?"

"Thank you."

"For what?"

"For not abandoning me out there."

Wyatt chuckled. "You know, Jordan, I'd love to take credit for that but that was all Billy."

Jordan nodded. "Still. Thank you."

Wyatt jabbed his finger at him, winked and rejoined

his family a few feet away. Catherine waited a second or two before walking over and wrapping an arm around his shoulders. "You ready to go, kiddo?"

He turned and gave her a big hug and for a few minutes they stood there in silence before turning back to the visitors center. "You know, mom, I was thinking maybe next year we could leave the tent behind and go on vacation to Miami. Somewhere near the beach, a hotel with a pool, and an all-you-can-eat buffet. What do you say?"

She paused for a second, looked around the park then replied, "As long as it has internet." Jordan shook his head and laughed as she hugged him tight..

* * *

THANK YOU FOR READING

The Year Without Summer

Please take a second to leave a review, it's really appreciated. Thanks kindly, Jack.

A Plea

Thank you for reading The Year Without Summer. If you enjoyed the book, I would really appreciate it if you would consider leaving a review. Without reviews, an author's books are virtually invisible on the retail sites. It also lets me know what you liked. You can leave a review by visiting the book's page. I would greatly appreciate it. It only takes a couple of seconds.

Thank you — **Jack Hunt**

Newsletter

Thank you for buying The Year Without Summer, published by Direct Response Publishing.

Click here to receive special offers, bonus content, and news about new Jack Hunt's books. Sign up for the newsletter. http://www.jackhuntbooks.com/signup/

About the Author

Jack Hunt is the author of horror, sci-fi and post-apocalyptic novels. He currently has three books out in the War Buds Series, Four books out in the EMP Survival series, Two books in the Against all Odds duology, Two books in the Wild Ones series, three in the Camp Zero series, five books out in the Renegades series, three books in the Agora Virus series, and several single novels. There is one called Blackout, one called Final Impact, one called Darkest Hour, one out in the Armada series, a time travel book called Killing Time and another called Mavericks: Hunters Moon. Jack lives on the East coast of North America.

Made in the USA
Lexington, KY
04 August 2019